The Faber Book
of Golden Fairytales

The Faber Book of

Golden Fairytales

SARA AND STEPHEN CORRIN

Illustrated by
Peter Melnyczuk

faber and faber
LONDON · BOSTON

First published in Great Britain in 1993
by Faber and Faber Limited
3 Queen Square London WC1N 3AU

Photoset by Parker Typesetting Service, Leicester
Printed in Great Britain by Clays Ltd, St Ives plc

A CIP record for this book is available from the British Library

ISBN: 0–571–16348–3

2 4 6 8 10 9 7 5 3 1

Contents

Acknowledgements

We are most grateful to the undermentioned authors, agents and publishers for permission to include the following stories:

James Riordan for *The Rosy Apple and the Golden Bowl* from *Tales from Central Russia* by James Riordan; Kestrel.

David Higham Associates for *Bertha Goldfoot* from *The Old Nurse's Stocking Basket* by Eleanor Farjeon, retold with permission in the third person; Oxford University Press. *The Golden Knucklebone* from *Cats and Creatures* by Ruth Manning-Sanders, Methuen. *The Nightingale and the Speck of Gold* (original title *The Nightingale*) from *The Iron Wolf and Other Stories* by Richard Adams; Kestrel.

Ginn and Co. Ltd and Beulah Candappa for *Greed for Gold* (original title *The Devil in Disguise*) from *Tales of South Asia*; Ginn.

Mary Martin and Eileen Colwell for *The Crock of Gold* from *The Princess Splendour and Other Stories* by Helen Waddell, edited by Eileen Colwell; Longman Young Books.

A. M. Heath and Joan Aiken for *The Golden-Fleeced Ram and the Hundred Elephants* from *The Kingdom Under the Sea* by Joan Aiken; Jonathan Cape.

Anna Wahlenberg for *Linda-Gold and the Old King* from *Swedish Fairy Tales*; The Bodley Head.

Every effort has been made to trace the authors of stories still in copyright but we apologize if there are any omissions.

We are much indebted to Eileen Colwell for her ever-ready help, and to the children's school librarians, who have helped us all along the line. And, of course, to Janice Thomson, children's books editor at Faber and Faber, we should like to express our gratitude for her tireless attention to detail and her sagacious guidance; without her this volume would not have made its appearance.

Sara and Stephen Corrin, 1993

A Word to the Storyteller

Gold possesses a magic lure for us all, far beyond its value as a precious metal. For centuries it has been an object of desire, but it is also a metaphor for what is desirable in man: purity, excellence and balance. We speak of 'a heart of gold', praise a well-behaved child for being 'as good as gold' and award gold medals for the highest achievements; we preach the golden rule and strive to practise the golden mean; we look for the golden opportunity that will transform our lives and we hark back to a supposed golden age when men and women lived in peace and harmony, and science, art and literature were in perfect balance. But there is a darker side to our fascination with gold. As much as it defines for us what we desire, it can also be an influence for evil.

The stories in this collection tell us much about the significance of gold in people's lives and how it shapes their fortunes for good and ill; how it can be a blessing and a curse. Linda-Gold is a girl with no riches but a golden heart who earns the blessing of a king. In 'The Nightingale and the Speck of Gold' God uses his last drop of gold paint to touch the bird's throat and give it a golden voice. The Happy Prince, moved by the poverty he can see from where he stands, a gold statue, high above the city, commands a little swallow to strip him of his inlaid gems and gold leaf and take them to the poor and needy; he loses his lustre and his fame, the swallow his life, but both have a reward in heaven.

'The Golden Goose' also tells of reward but it introduces a note of warning. Simpleton earns a golden goose for his kindness to a dwarf but those who try to steal it from him are punished. This theme is ubiquitous in myth and fairytale and indeed many of these stories are cautionary tales. In the powerful legend 'Andvari's Gold' a dread curse becomes inseparable from the stolen hoard of treasure and he, Andvari, recalls the prophecy of the Norns: 'To those wise beings who fashion the world gold is the seed of further gold and unseen glory but to wasteful men it is the certain seed of woe and grief for generations yet to come.'

Another wise proverb cautions that gold may be bought too dear – a lesson that King Midas learns when he is granted the power to change everything he touches into gold. When he unwittingly embraces his daughter and turns her into a cold and glistening statue he realizes in his grief that gold can demand too great a sacrifice. All that glitters is indeed not gold, yet throughout the ages men have been driven by their desire to possess it. Some, like Jason in his quest for the golden fleece, are driven to deeds of heroism; others to deeds of infamy and murder, as in 'Greed for Gold'.

But whether a force for good or evil, whether reward or curse, gold and what it symbolizes is central to many of our most enduring fairytales. They themselves are treasures, and here is a selection – to be discovered and enjoyed simply in the telling.

The Golden Key

In the heart of winter when the ground was covered with a thick carpet of snow a poor young lad had to go out on a sledge and bring back some wood. When he had piled up what he thought was enough, he felt so freezingly cold he decided that before trudging back home he would make a fire to warm himself up a bit. But when he had cleared away the snow to make space for his little fire, he found a small golden key. Now where there's a key there's bound to be a lock, thought the lad. So he began digging into the earth and before long he came upon a small iron chest. If only the key fits the lock, he thought, there must surely be some precious things in this chest. He searched all over the chest and all around it but could find no key-hole. At long last, however, he did find one but it was so tiny you could scarcely see it. He tried the key and what do you think? The key fitted exactly. He turned the key round and lifted up the lid . . . and now we'll learn what wonderful treasures it contained . . .

The Golden Goose

There was once a man who had three sons. The youngest was called Dummling. He was mocked and scorned by the others who at every opportunity tried to put him down. Now it happened that the eldest was one day going into the forest to cut wood and before he set off his mother gave him a delicious pancake and a bottle of wine so that he shouldn't get too hungry or thirsty. Just as he got into the forest he met a little grey old man who bade him good-day and said, 'Give me a piece of your pancake and a drop of your wine – I'm so hungry and thirsty.' This clever young man, however, replied, 'If I were to give you some of my cake and wine, I'd have little left for myself. Be off with you!' And he left the man standing there and continued on his way.

When he began to hew down a tree it wasn't long before he missed his aim and his axe cut into his arm so that he had to go back home to have it bandaged. It was the little old man who had been at the bottom of this accident.

And now the second son went to the forest, his mother again giving him a pancake and a bottle of wine, and likewise *he* was met by the little old grey man who asked him for some of his pancake and wine. And thinking himself very clever he said, 'What I give you will be that much less left for me,' and he went on his way, leaving the little man where he stood. His punishment wasn't long in coming for before he'd made only two cuts in the tree he wounded himself in the leg and had to go home to be seen to.

Then Dummling said, 'Father, let me go into the woods to hew some wood,' but his father refused, saying, 'Your brothers have both injured themselves, so you'd be better off staying at home, for you are quite useless at it.' But Dummling was so persistent that finally his father said, 'Very well then, go and perhaps the experience might make you a little wiser.' But his mother gave him only a small cake which she baked over some warm ashes and a bottle of sour beer. The little old grey man met him with the same request: 'Give me some of your cake and a sip of your drink, I'm so hungry and thirsty.' Dummling replied, 'I've only got some ash-baked cake and a bottle of sour beer, but if that suits you let's sit down and eat.'

So they sat down and when Dummling got out his cake, lo! it had turned into a delicious pancake and the sour beer into a fine wine. They ate and drank and when they had finished, the little man said, 'Since you have a kind heart and have willingly shared what you had, I will make you lucky. Over there stands an old tree, cut it down and you will find something at the roots.' Thereupon the little man took his leave.

Dummling went off to the tree and cut it down and when it fell, there among the roots sat a goose whose feathers were of pure gold. He picked it up and carried it with him to an inn where he thought he would spend the night.

The landlord had three daughters and when they saw the goose they were most curious about this wonderful bird and wanted to pluck one of its feathers. The eldest daughter thought, I'll soon find an opportunity to get hold of one, and as soon as Dummling had gone out she seized the goose by its wing but found that her finger and thumb were stuck fast on it so she couldn't get away. Soon after, the second daughter came along with no other intention but to get hold of a golden feather but scarcely had she touched her sister when she found herself held fast. At last the third sister arrived with the same thought in mind, but the other two cried out, 'Keep away! Keep away! For heaven's sake, keep away!' But she couldn't understand why she should and thought, Why, if they are there, shouldn't I be there too? Springing up to them she touched her sister and was at

[3]

once stuck fast to her. So all three had to pass the night with the goose.

Next morning Dummling took the goose under his arm without even bothering about the three girls who were still hanging on and were obliged to keep running, now left now right, wherever Dummling's legs carried him. In the middle of a field the parson met them and when he saw the little procession he cried out, 'Aren't you ashamed of yourselves, you wicked girls, to run after a young man across the fields like this! Is that proper?' So saying he took the youngest by the hand to try to pull her away but the second he touched her he, too, was stuck fast and had to join the procession. Shortly after up came the verger and saw his master following the three girls. Much astonished by the sight, he called out, 'I say, Your Reverence, where are you off to so fast? Don't forget, we have a christening on today.' He caught up with them and grabbed hold of his gown and found himself stuck fast.

As the five of them went trotting along they met two labourers coming back from the fields holding their hatchets in their hands. The parson called out to them and begged them to come and set him and the verger free. But no sooner had they touched the verger than they too stuck fast to him and so now there were seven of them, all led by Dummling carrying his goose.

By and by he came to a city ruled by a king whose only daughter was so serious and solemn that nobody at all could make her laugh. So the king had issued a decree that whoever *could* make her laugh should have her as his wife. When Dummling heard of this he carried his Golden Goose, with all his procession following, in front of the princess and as soon as she saw all those seven people trotting behind him she burst into such a fit of hearty laughter that it seemed as though it would never stop. Then Dummling claimed her as his wife, the marriage was celebrated and they lived long and happily together.

The King of the Golden River

I

In a secluded and mountainous part of Stiria there was, in old time, a valley of the most surprising and luxuriant fertility. It was surrounded, on all sides, by steep and rocky mountains, rising into peaks, which were always covered with snow, and from which a number of torrents descended in constant cataracts. One of these fell westward, over the face of a crag so high, that, when the sun had set to everything else, and all below was darkness, his beams still shone full upon this waterfall, so that it looked like a shower of gold. It was, therefore, called by the people of the neighbourhood, the Golden River. The clouds were drawn so constantly to the snowy hills, and rested so softly in the circular hollow, that in time of drought and heat, when all the country round was burnt up, there was still rain in the little valley; and its crops were so heavy, and its hay so high, and its apples so red, and its grapes so blue, and its wine so rich, and its honey so sweet, that it was a marvel to everyone who beheld it and was commonly called the Treasure Valley.

The whole of this valley belonged to three brothers, called Schwartz, Hans and Gluck. Schwartz and Hans, the two elder brothers, were very ugly men, with overhanging eyebrows, and

[5]

small dull eyes, which were always half shut, so that you couldn't see into them. They lived by farming the Treasure Valley, and very good farmers they were. They killed everything that did not pay for its eating. They shot the blackbirds, because they pecked the fruit, and poisoned the crickets for eating the crumbs in the kitchen. They worked their servants without any wages, till they would not work any more, and then quarrelled with them, and turned them out of doors without paying them. It would have been very odd, if with such a farm, and such a system of farming, they hadn't got very rich; and very rich they did get. They generally contrived to keep their corn by them till it was very dear, and then sell it for twice its value; they had heaps of gold lying about on their floors, yet it was never known that they had given so much as a penny in charity; and they grumbled perpetually at paying tithes; they were, in a word, of so cruel and grinding a temper, as to receive from all those with whom they had any dealings, the nickname of the Two Rascals.

The youngest brother, Gluck, was as completely opposed, in both appearance and character, to his seniors as could possibly be imagined. He was not above twelve years old, fair, blue-eyed, and kind in temper to every living thing. He did not, of course, agree particularly well with his brothers, and was usually appointed to the honourable office of turnspit, when there was anything to roast, which was not often; for, to do the brothers justice, they were hardly less sparing upon themselves than upon other people. Gluck had to clean the plates, occasionally getting what was left on them, by way of encouragement, and a wholesome quantity of dry blows, by way of education.

Things went on in this manner for a long time. At last came a very wet summer, and everything went wrong in the country around. The hay had hardly been got in, when the haystacks were floated bodily down to the sea by a flood; the vines were cut to pieces with the hail; the corn was all killed by blight; only in the Treasure Valley, as usual, all was safe. As it had rain when there was rain nowhere else, so it had sun when there was sun nowhere else. Everybody came to buy corn at the farm, and went away pouring curses on the Two Rascals. They asked what they liked, and got it, except from the poor people, who could only beg, and several of whom were starved at their very door, without the slightest regard or notice.

It was drawing towards winter, and very cold weather, when one

[6]

day the two elder brothers had gone out, with their usual warning to little Gluck, who was left to mind the roast, that he was to let nobody in, and give nothing out. Gluck sat down quite close to the fire, for it was raining very hard, and the kitchen walls were by no means dry or comfortable looking. He turned and turned, and the roast got nice and brown. What a pity, thought Gluck, my brothers never ask anybody to dinner. I'm sure, when they've got such a nice piece of mutton as this, and nobody else has got so much as a piece of dry bread, it would do their hearts good to have somebody to eat it with them.

Just as he spoke, there came a double knock at the house door, heavy and dull, as though the knocker had been tied up – more like a puff than a knock.

'It must be the wind,' said Gluck, 'nobody else would venture to knock double knocks at our door.'

No, it wasn't the wind; there it came again very hard, and what was particularly astounding, the knocker seemed to be in a hurry, and not to be in the least afraid of the consequences. Gluck went to the window, opened it, and put his head out to see who it was.

It was the most extraordinary looking little gentleman he had ever seen in his life. He had a very large nose, slightly brass-coloured; his cheeks were very round, and very red, and might have warranted a supposition that he had been blowing the dying embers of a fire for the last eight and forty hours; his eyes twinkled merrily through long silky eyelashes, his moustaches curled twice round like a corkscrew on each side of his mouth, and his hair, of a curious mixed pepper-and-salt colour, descended far over his shoulders. He was about four-foot six in height, and wore a conical pointed cap nearly as tall as himself, decorated with a black feather some three feet long. His doublet trailed behind him like a swallow tail, but it was hidden by an enormous black, glossy-looking cloak, which must have been very much too long in calm weather, as the wind, now whistling round the old house, carried it clear out from the wearer's shoulders to about four times his own length.

Gluck was so perfectly paralysed by the very unusual appearance of his visitor, that he remained fixed without uttering a word, until the old gentleman, having performed another musical tapping on the knocker, turned round to look after his fly-away cloak. In doing so he caught sight of Gluck's little yellow head jammed in the window, with its mouth and eyes very wide open indeed.

'Hallo!' said the little gentleman, 'That's no the way to answer the door. I'm wet, let me in.'

To do the little gentleman justice, he was wet. His feather hung down between his legs like a beaten puppy's tail, dripping like an umbrella, and from the ends of his moustaches water was running into his waistcoat pockets, and out again like a mill stream.

'I beg pardon, sir,' said Gluck, 'I'm very sorry, but I really can't.'

'Can't what?' said the old gentleman.

'I can't let you in, sir – I can't indeed; my brothers would beat me to death, sir, if I thought of such a thing. What do you want, sir?'

'Want?' said the old gentleman, petulantly. 'I want fire, and shelter; and there's your great fire there blazing, crackling, and dancing on the walls, with nobody to feel it. Let me in, I say; I only want to warm myself.'

Gluck had his head, by this time, so long out of the window, that he began to feel it was really unpleasantly cold, and when he turned, and saw the beautiful fire rustling and roaring, and throwing long bright tongues up the chimney, as if it were licking its chops at the savoury smell of the leg of mutton, his heart melted within him that it should be burning away for nothing. 'He does look very wet,' said little Gluck, 'I'll just let him in for a quarter of an hour.' Round he went to the door, and opened it; and as the little gentleman walked in, there came a gust of wind through the house, that made the old chimneys totter.

'That's a good boy,' said the little gentleman. 'Never mind your brothers. I'll talk to them.'

'Pray, sir, don't do any such thing,' said Gluck. 'I can't let you stay till they come; they'd be the death of me.'

'Dear me,' said the old gentleman, 'I'm very sorry to hear that. How long may I stay?'

'Only till the mutton's done, sir,' replied Gluck, 'and it's very brown.'

Then the old gentleman walked into the kitchen, and sat himself down on the hob, with the top of his cap fitting neatly into the chimney.

'You'll soon dry there, sir,' said Gluck, and sat down again to turn the mutton. But the old gentleman did not dry there, but went on to drip, drip, dripping among the cinders, and the fire fizzed, and sputtered, and began to look very black, and uncomfortable: never was such a cloak; every fold in it ran like a gutter.

[8]

'I beg pardon, sir,' said Gluck at length, after watching the water spreading in long, quicksilver-like streams over the floor for a quarter of an hour; 'mayn't I take your cloak?'

'No, thank you,' said the old gentleman.

'Your cap, sir?'

'I'm all right, thank you,' said the old gentleman rather gruffly.

'But, – sir – I'm very sorry,' said Gluck, hesitatingly; 'but – really, sir – you're – putting the fire out.'

'It'll take longer to do the mutton, then,' replied his visitor drily.

Gluck was very much puzzled by the behaviour of his guest; it was such a strange mixture of coolness and politeness. He turned away at the spit thoughtfully for another five minutes.

'That mutton looks very nice,' said the old gentleman at length. 'Can't you give me a little bit?'

'Impossible, sir,' said Gluck.

'I'm very hungry,' continued the old gentleman; 'I've had nothing to eat yesterday, nor today. They surely couldn't miss a bit from the knuckle!'

He spoke in so very melancholy a tone, that it quite melted Gluck's heart. 'They promised me one slice today, sir,' said he; 'I can give you that, but not a bit more.'

'That's a good boy,' said the old gentleman again.

Then Gluck warmed a plate, and sharpened a knife. I don't care if I do get beaten for it, thought he. Just as he had cut a large slice out of the mutton, there came a tremendous rap at the door. The old gentleman jumped off the hob, as if it had suddenly become inconveniently warm. Gluck fitted the slice into the mutton again, with desperate efforts to fit it back exactly and ran to open the door.

'What did you keep us waiting in the rain for?' asked Schwartz, as he walked in, throwing his umbrella in Gluck's face. 'Ay! what for, indeed, you little vagabond?' said Hans, administering an educational box on the ear, as he followed his brother into the kitchen.

'Bless my soul!' said Schwartz when he opened the door.

'Amen,' said the little gentleman, who had taken his cap off, and was standing in the middle of the kitchen, bowing rapidly over and over again.

'Who's that?' said Schwartz, catching a rolling-pin, and turning to Gluck with a fierce frown.

'I don't know, indeed, brother,' said Gluck in great terror.

[9]

'How did he get in?' roared Schwartz.

'My dear brother,' said Gluck, apologetically, 'he was so very wet!'

The rolling-pin was descending on Gluck's head, but, at the instant, the old gentleman pushed his conical cap in between, on which it crashed with a shock that shook the water out of it all over the room. What was very odd, the rolling-pin no sooner touched the cap than it flew out of Schwartz's hand, spinning like a straw in a high wind, and fell into the corner at the further end of the room.

'Who are you, sir?' demanded Schwartz, turning upon him.

'What's your business?' snarled Hans.

'I'm a poor old man, sir,' the little gentleman began very modestly, 'and I saw your fire through the window, and begged shelter for a quarter of an hour.'

'Have the goodness to walk out again, then,' said Schwartz. 'We've quite enough water in our kitchen, without making it a drying-house.'

'It is a cold day to turn an old man out in, sir; look at my grey hairs.' They hung down to his shoulders, as I told you before.

'Ay!' said Hans, 'there are enough of them to keep you warm. Walk!'

'I'm very, very hungry, sir; couldn't you spare me a bit of bread before I go?'

'Bread, indeed!' said Schwartz; 'do you suppose we've nothing to do with our bread but to give it to such a red-nosed fellow as you?'

'Why don't you sell your feather?' said Hans, sneeringly. 'Out with you!'

'A little bit,' said the old gentleman.

'Be off!' said Schwartz.

'Pray, gentlemen.'

'Off,' shrieked Hans, seizing him by the collar. But he had no sooner touched the old gentleman's collar, than away he went after the rolling-pin, spinning round and round, till he fell into the corner on the top of it. Then Schwartz was very angry, and ran at the old gentleman to turn him out; but he also had hardly touched him, when away he went after Hans and the rolling-pin, and hit his head against the wall as he tumbled into the corner. And so there they lay, all three.

Then the old gentleman spun himself round speedily in the opposite direction; continued to spin until his long cloak was wound neatly about him; clapped his cap on his head, very much on one side (for it could not stand upright without going through the ceiling), gave an additional twist to his corkscrew moustaches, and replied with perfect coolness: 'Gentlemen, I wish you a very good morning. At twelve o'clock tonight I'll call again; after such a refusal of hospitality as I have just experienced, you will not be surprised if that visit is the last I ever pay you.'

'If I ever catch you here again,' muttered Schwartz, coming, half-frightened, out of the corner – but, before he could finish his sentence, the old gentleman had shut the door behind him with a great bang.

'A very pretty business, indeed, Mr Gluck!' said Schwartz. 'Dish the mutton, sir. If I ever catch you at such a trick again – bless me, why the mutton's been cut!'

'You promised me one slice, brother, you know,' said Gluck.

'Oh! and you were cutting it hot, I suppose, and going to catch all the gravy. It'll be long before I promise you such a thing again. Leave the room, sir; and have the kindness to wait in the coal cellar till I call you.'

Gluck left the room melancholy enough. The brothers ate as much mutton as they could, locked the rest in the cupboard, and proceeded to get very drunk after dinner.

The brothers had just sense enough left to put up all the shutters, and double-bar the door, before they went to bed. They usually slept in the same room. As the clock struck twelve, they were both awakened by a tremendous crash. Their door burst open with a violence that shook the house from top to bottom.

'What's that?' cried Schwartz, starting up in his bed.

'Only I,' said the little gentleman.

The two brothers sat up on their bolster, and stared into the darkness. The room was full of water and, by a misty moonbeam, which found its way through a hole in the shutter, they could see in the midst of it an enormous foam globe spinning round, and bobbing up and down like a cork on which, as on a most luxurious cushion, lay the little gentleman, cap and all. There was plenty of room for it now as the roof was off.

'Sorry to inconvenience you,' said their visitor, ironically. 'I'm afraid your beds are dampish; perhaps you had better go to your brother's room: I've left the ceiling on, there.'

They required no second warning, but rushed into Gluck's room wet through, and in an agony of terror.

'You'll find my card on the kitchen table,' the old gentleman called after them. 'Remember, the *last* visit.'

'Pray Heaven it may be!' said Schwartz, shuddering. And the foam globe disappeared.

Dawn came at last, and the two brothers looked out of Gluck's little window in the morning. The Treasure Valley was one mass of ruin and desolation. The flood had swept away trees, crops, and cattle, and left in their stead a waste of red sand and grey mud. The two brothers crept shivering and horror-struck into the kitchen. The water had gutted the whole first floor: corn, money, almost every movable thing had been swept away, and there was left only a small white card on the kitchen table. On it, in large, breezy, long-legged letters, were engraved the words:

II

South-West Wind, Esquire was as good as his word. After the hair-raising visit above related, he entered the Treasure Valley no more; and, what was worse, he had so much influence with his relations, the West Winds in general, that they all adopted a similar line of conduct. So no rain fell in the valley from one year's end to another. Though everything remained green and flourishing in the plains below, the land of the Three Brothers was a desert. What had once been the richest soil in the kingdom became a shifting heap of red sand; and the brothers were forced to abandon their valueless fields in despair, to seek some means of gaining a livelihood among the cities and people of the plains. All their money was gone, and they had nothing left but some curious old-fashioned pieces of gold plate, the last remnants of their ill-gotten wealth.

'Suppose we turn goldsmiths?' said Schwartz to Hans, as they entered the large city. 'It is a good trade for us; we can put a great deal of copper into the gold, without anyone's finding it out.'

The thought was agreed to be a very good one; they hired a furnace, and turned goldsmiths. But two slight circumstances affected their trade: the first, that people did not approve of the coppered gold; the second, that the two elder brothers, whenever they had sold anything, used to leave little Gluck to mind the furnace, and go and drink out the money in the ale-house next door. So they melted all their gold, without making any money to buy more, and were at last reduced to one large drinking mug, which an uncle of his had given to little Gluck, and which he was very fond of, and would not have parted with for the world; though he never drank anything out of it but milk and water. The mug was a very odd mug to look at. The handle was formed of two wreaths of flowing golden hair, so finely spun that it looked more like silk than metal, and these wreaths descended into, and mixed with, a beard and whiskers of the same exquisite workmanship, which surrounded and decorated a very fierce little face, of the reddest gold imaginable, right in front of the mug, with a pair of eyes in it which seemed to see all the way round it. It was impossible to drink out of the mug without being subjected to an intense gaze out of the side of these eyes; Schwartz positively declared that once, after emptying it, full of Rhenish, seventeen times, he had seen them wink! When it came to the mug's turn to be made into spoons, it half broke poor little Gluck's heart, but the brothers only laughed at him, tossed the mug into the melting-pot, and staggered out to the ale-house; leaving him, as usual, to pour the gold into bars, when it was all ready.

When they were gone, Gluck took a farewell look at his old friend in the melting-pot. The flowing hair was all gone; nothing remained but the red nose, and the sparkling eyes, which looked more mischievous than ever And no wonder, thought Gluck, after being treated in that way. He wandered gloomily over to the window, and sat himself down to catch the fresh evening air, and escape the hot breath of the furnace. Now this window commanded a direct view of the range of mountains, which, as I told you before, overhung the Treasure Valley, and more especially of the peak from which fell the Golden River. It was just at the close of the day, and when Gluck sat down at the window, he saw the rocks of the mountain tops, all crimson and purple with the sunset; and there were bright tongues of fiery cloud burning and quivering about them; and the river, brighter than all, fell, a waving column of pure gold, from precipice to precipice, with the double arch of a broad purple rainbow stretched across.

'Ah!' said Gluck aloud, after he had looked at it for a while, 'if that river were really all gold, what a nice thing it would be.'

'No, it wouldn't, Gluck,' said a clear metallic voice, close at his ear.

'Bless me, what's that?' exclaimed Gluck, jumping up. There was nobody there. He looked round the room, and under the table, and a great many times behind him, but there was certainly nobody there, and he sat down again at the window. This time he didn't speak, but he couldn't help thinking again that it would be very convenient if the river were really all gold.

'Not at all, my boy,' said the same voice, louder than before.

'Bless me!' said Gluck again, 'what is that?' He looked again into all the corners, and cupboards, and then began turning round, and round, as fast as he could in the middle of the room, thinking there was somebody behind him, when the same voice struck again on his ear. It was singing now very merrily, 'Lala – lira – la'; no words, only a soft running bubbly melody, something like that of a kettle on the boil. Gluck looked out of the window. No, it was certainly in the house. Upstairs, and downstairs. No, it was certainly in that very room, coming in quicker time, and clearer notes, every moment. 'Lala – lira – la.' All at once it struck Gluck that is sounded louder near the furnace. He ran to the opening and looked in: yes, he was right, it seemed to be coming, not only out of the furnace, but out of the pot. He uncovered it, and ran back in a great fright, for the pot was certainly singing! He stood in the farthest corner of the room, with his hands up, and his mouth open, for a minute or two, when the singing stopped, and the voice became clear.

'Hallo!' said the voice.

Gluck made no answer.

'Hallo! Gluck, my boy,' said the pot again.

Gluck summoned all his energies, walked straight up to the melting-pot, drew it out of the furnace, and looked in. The gold was all melted, and its surface as smooth and polished as a river; but instead of reflecting little Gluck's head, as he looked in, he saw meeting his glance from beneath the gold, the red nose, and sharp eyes of his old friend the mug, a thousand times redder, and sharper than ever he had seen them in his life.

'Come, Gluck, my boy,' said the voice out of the pot again, 'I'm all right; pour me out.'

But Gluck was much too astonished to do anything of the kind.

'Pour me out, I say,' said the voice rather gruffly.

Still Gluck didn't move.

'Will you pour me out?' said the voice passionately, 'I'm too hot.'

By a violent effort, Gluck recovered the use of his limbs, took hold of

[15]

the melting-pot and tipped it, so as to pour out the gold. But instead of a liquid stream, there came out, first, a pair of pretty little yellow legs, then some coat-tails, then a pair of arms stuck akimbo, and finally, the well-known head of his friend the mug; all of which parts uniting as they rolled out, stood up energetically on the floor, in the shape of a little golden dwarf, about a foot and a half high.

'That's right!' said the dwarf, stretching out first his legs, and then his arms, and then shaking his head up and down, as far round as it would go for five minutes, without stopping, apparently with the view of making sure if he were quite correctly put together, while Gluck stood staring at him in speechless amazement. He was dressed in a doublet of spun gold, so fine in its texture that the colours gleamed over it, as if on a surface of mother-of-pearl, and over this brilliant doublet, his hair and beard fell full half way to the ground, in waving curls, so exquisitely delicate, that Gluck could hardly tell where they ended; they seemed to melt into air. The features of the face, however, were by no means finished with the same delicacy; they were rather coarse, slightly coppery in complexion, and indicative, in expression of a very stubborn disposition in his little personage. When the dwarf had finished his self-examination, he turned his small sharp eyes full on Gluck, and stared at him deliberately for a minute or two. 'No, it wouldn't, Gluck, my boy,' said the little man.

This was certainly rather an abrupt, unconnected mode of commencing conversation, but Gluck had no inclination to argue the points.

'Wouldn't it, sir?' said Gluck, very mildly and submissively indeed.

'No,' said the dwarf, conclusively. 'No, it wouldn't.' And with that, the dwarf pulled his cap hard over his brows, and took two turns up and down the room, lifting his legs very high, and setting them down very hard. This pause gave time for Gluck to collect his thoughts a little, and, seeing no great reason to view his diminutive visitor with dread, and feeling his curiosity overcome his amazement, he ventured a question of peculiar delicacy.

'Pray, sir,' said Gluck, rather hesitatingly, 'were you my mug?'

On which the little man turned sharp round, walked straight up to Gluck, and drew himself up to his full height. 'I', said the little man, 'am the King of the Golden River.'

'I hope Your Majesty is very well,' said Gluck, determined to say something.

'Listen!' said the little man, deigning no reply to this polite enquiry. 'I am the King of what you mortals call the Golden River. What I have seen of you, and your conduct to your wicked brothers, renders me willing to serve you; therefore, attend to what I tell you. Whoever shall climb to the top of that mountain from which you see the Golden River flowing, and shall cast into the stream at its source three drops of holy water: for him, and for him only, the river shall turn to gold. But no one failing in his first attempt can succeed in a second; and if any one shall cast unholy water into the river, it will overwhelm him, and he will become a black stone.'

So saying, the King of the Golden River turned away and deliberately walked into the centre of the hottest flame of the furnace. His figure became red, white, transparent, dazzling – a blaze of intense light – rose, trembled, and disappeared. The King of the Golden River had evaporated.

'Oh!' cried poor Gluck, running to look up the chimney after him; 'Oh, dear, dear, dear me! My mug! my mug! my mug!'

III

The King of the Golden River had hardly made the extraordinary exit already described, before Hans and Schwartz came roaring into the house, very savagely drunk. The discovery of the total loss of their last piece of gold plate had the effect of sobering them just enough to enable them to stand over Gluck, beating him very steadily for a quarter of an hour, at the end of which period they dropped into a couple of chairs, and requested to know what he had got to say for himself. Gluck told them his story, of which, of course, they did not believe a word. They beat him again, till their arms were tired, and staggered to bed. In the morning, however, the steadiness with which he stuck to his story made them begin to believe him, the immediate consequence of which was that the two brothers, after wrangling a long time on the knotty question which of them should try his fortune first, drew their swords and began fighting. The noise of the fray alarmed the neighbours, who, finding they could not separate the combatants, sent for the constable.

Hans, on hearing this, contrived to escape and hid himself, but Schwartz was taken before the magistrate, fined for breaking the peace, and, having drunk out his last penny the evening before, was thrown into prison till he should pay.

[17]

When Hans heard this, he was much delighted, and determined to set out immediately for the Golden River. How to get the holy water, was the question. He went to the priest, but the priest could not give any holy water to so unholy a character. So Hans went to vespers in the evening for the first time in his life, and, under pretence of crossing himself, stole a cupful, and returned home in triumph.

Next morning he got up before the sun rose, put the holy water into a strong flask, and two bottles of wine and some meat in a basket, slung them over his back, took his alpine staff in his hand, and set off for the mountains.

On his way out of the town he had to pass the prison, and as he looked in at the windows, whom should he see but Schwartz himself peeping out of the bars, and looking very miserable.

'Good morning, brother,' said Hans, 'have you any message for the King of the Golden River?'

Schwartz gnashed his teeth with rage, and shook the bars with all his strength, but Hans only laughed at him, and advising him to make himself comfortable till he came back again, shouldered his basket, shook the bottle of holy water in Schwartz's face till it frothed again, and marched off in the highest spirits in the world.

It was, indeed, a morning that might have made anyone happy, even with no Golden River to seek for. Level lines of dewy mist lay stretched along the valley, out of which rose the massy mountains. Far above shot up red splintered masses of castellated rock, jagged and shivered into thousands of fantastic forms, with here and there a streak of sunlit snow traced down their chasms like a line of forked lightning; and, far beyond, and far above all these, slept, in the blue sky, the utmost peaks of the eternal snow.

The Golden River, which sprang from one of the lower and snowless elevations, was now nearly in shadow.

On this object, and on this alone, Hans's eyes and thoughts were fixed; forgetting the distance he had to traverse, he set off at too fast a rate of walking, which greatly exhausted him before he had scaled the first range of the green and low hills. He was, moreover, surprised, on surmounting them, to find that a large glacier, of whose existence, despite his previous knowledge of the mountains, he had been absolutely ignorant, lay between him and the source of the Golden River. He entered on it with the boldness of a practised mountaineer; yet he thought he had never crossed so strange or dangerous a glacier in his life. The ice was excessively slippery, and out of all its chasms came wild sounds of gushing water; not monotonous or low, but changeful and loud, rising occasionally into passages of wild melody, then breaking off into short melancholy tones, or sudden shrieks, resembling those of human voices in distress or pain. Myriads of deceitful shadows and lurid lights played and floated about dazzling and confusing the sight of the traveller, while his ears grew dull and his head giddy with the constant gush and roar of the concealed waters. These painful circumstances grew worse, as he went on. The ice crashed and yawned into fresh chasms at his feet, tottering spires nodded around him, and fell thundering across his path; and though he had repeatedly faced these dangers on the most terrific glaciers, and in the wildest weather, it was with a new and oppressive feeling of panic terror that he leaped the last chasm, and flung himself, exhausted and shuddering, on the firm turf of the mountain.

He had been compelled to abandon his basket of food, which became a perilous burden on the glacier, and had now no means of refreshing himself but by breaking off and eating some of the pieces of ice. This, however, relieved his thirst; an hour's rest restored his strength and with the indomitable spirit of greed he resumed his laborious journey.

His way now lay straight up a ridge of bare red rocks, without a blade of grass to ease the foot, or a projecting angle to afford an inch of shade from the south sun. It was past noon, and the rays beat intensely upon the steep path, while the whole atmosphere was still and penetrated with heat. Intense thirst was soon added to the bodily fatigue with which Hans was now afflicted; glance after glance he cast on the flask of water which hung at his belt. 'Three drops are enough,' at last thought he. 'I may, at least, cool my lips with it.'

He opened the flask, and was raising it to his lips, when his eye fell on an object lying on the rock beside him; he thought it moved. It was a small dog, apparently in the last agony of death from thirst. Its tongue was out, its jaws dry, it limbs extended lifelessly, and a swarm of black ants were crawling about its lips and throat. Its eye moved to the bottle which Hans held in his hand. He raised it, drank, kicked the animal with his foot, and passed on. And he did not know how it was, but he thought that a strange shadow had suddenly come across the blue sky.

The path became steeper and more rugged every moment, and the high hill air, instead of refreshing him, seemed to throw his blood into a fever. His thirst increased every moment. Another hour passed, and he again looked down to the flask at his side; it was half empty; but there was much more than three drops in it. He stopped to open it, and again, as he did so, something moved in the path above him. It was a fair child, stretched nearly lifeless on the rock, its breast heaving with thirst, its eyes closed, and its lips parched and burning. Hans eyed it deliberately, drank, and passed on. And a dark grey cloud came over the sun, and long, snake-like shadows crept up along the mountain sides. Hans struggled on. The sun was sinking, but its descent seemed to bring no coolness; the leaden weight of the dead air pressed upon his brow and heart, but the goal was near. He saw the cataract of the Golden River springing from the hillside, scarcely five hundred feet above him. He paused for a moment to breathe, and sprang on to complete his task.

At this instant a faint cry fell on his ear. He turned, and saw a grey-haired old man extended on the rocks. His eyes were shrunk, his features deadly pale, and gathered into an expression of despair. 'Water!' he stretched his arms to Hans, and cried feebly, 'Water! I am dying.'

'I have none,' replied Hans, 'you have had your share of life.' He strode over the old man's body, and darted on. And a flash of blue lightning rose out of the East, shaped like a sword; it shook three times over the whole heaven, and left it dark with one heavy, impenetrable shade. The sun was setting; it plunged towards the horizon like a red-hot ball.

The roar of the Golden River rose on Hans's ear. He stood at the brink of the chasm through which it ran. Its waves were filled with the red glory of the sunset: they shook their crests like tongues of fire, and flashes of bloody light gleamed along their foam. Their sound came mightier and mightier on his senses and his brain grew giddy. Shuddering he drew the flask from his girdle, and hurled it into the centre of the torrent. As he did so, an icy chill shot through his limbs: he staggered, shrieked and fell. The waters closed over his cry. And the moaning of the river rose wildly into the night, as it gushed over
THE BLACK STONE . . .

IV

Poor little Gluck waited very anxiously alone in the house for Hans's return, Finding he did not come back, he was terribly frightened, and went and told Schwartz in the prison all that had happened. Then Schwartz was very much pleased, and said that Hans must certainly have been turned into a black stone, and he should have all the gold to himself. But Gluck was very sorry, and cried all night. When he got up in the morning, there was no bread in the house, nor any money; so Gluck went and hired himself to another goldsmith, and he worked so hard, and so long every day, that he soon got money enough to pay his brother's fine, and he went and gave it all to Schwartz, and Schwartz got out of prison. Then Schwartz was quite pleased, and said he should have some of the gold of the river. But Gluck only begged he would go and see what had become of Hans.

Now when Schwartz heard that Hans had stolen the holy water, he thought to himself that such conduct might not be considered altogether correct by the King of the Golden River, and determined to manage matters better. So he took some more of Gluck's money, and went to a bad priest, who gave him some holy water very readily for it. Then Schwartz was sure it was all quite right. So Schwartz got up early in the morning before the sun rose, and took some bread and wine, in a basket, and put his holy water in a flask, and set off for the mountains. Like his brother he was much surprised at the sight of the glacier, and had great difficulty in crossing it, even after leaving his basket behind him. The day was cloudless, but not bright: there was a heavy purple haze hanging over the sky, and the hills looked lowering and gloomy. And as Schwartz climbed the steep rock path, the thirst came upon him, as it had upon his brother, until he lifted his flask to his lips to drink. Then he saw the fair child lying near him on the rocks, and it cried to him, and moaned for water.

'Water, indeed,' said Schwartz, 'I haven't half enough for myself,' and passed on. And as he went he thought the sunbeams grew more dim, and he saw a low bank of black cloud rising out of the West, and when he had climbed for another hour the thirst overcame him again, and he would have drunk. Then he saw the old man lying before him on the path, and heard him cry for water. 'Water, indeed,' said Schwartz, 'I haven't half enough for myself,' and on he went.

Then again the light seemed to fade from before his eyes, and he looked up, and behold, a mist of the colour of blood had come over the sun, and the bank of black cloud had risen very high, and its edges were tossing and tumbling like the waves of the angry sea. And they cast long shadows, which flickered over Schwartz's path.

Then Schwartz climbed for another hour, and again his thirst returned; as he lifted his flask to his lips, he thought he saw his brother Hans lying exhausted on the path before him, and, as he gazed, the figure stretched its arms to him, and cried for water. 'Ha, ha,' laughed Schwartz, 'are you there? Remember the prison bars, my boy. Water, indeed! do you suppose I carried it all the way up here for you?' And he strode over the figure; yet, as he passed, he thought he saw a strange expression of mockery about its lips. And when he had gone a few yards farther, he looked back; but the figure was not there.

And a sudden horror came over Schwartz, he did not know why; but the thirst for gold proved stronger than his fear, and he rushed on. And the bank of black clouds rose to the zenith, and out of it came bursts of lightning, and waves of darkness seemed to heave and float between their flashes, over the whole heavens. And the sky where the sun was setting was like a lake of blood; and a strong wind came out of that sky, tearing its crimson clouds into fragments, and scattering them far into the darkness. And when Schwartz stood by the brink of the Golden River, its waves were black, like thunder clouds, but their foam was like fire; and the roar of the waters below and the thunder above met as he cast the flask into the stream. And, as he did so, the lightning glared in his eyes, and the earth gave way beneath him, and the waters closed over his cry. And the moaning of the river rose wildly into the night, as it gushed over the TWO BLACK STONES . . .

V

When Gluck found that Schwartz did not come back, he was very sorry, and did not know what to do. He had no money, and was obliged to go and hire himself again to the goldsmith, who worked him very hard, and gave him very little money. So, after a month or two, Gluck grew tired, and made up his mind to go and try his fortune with the Golden River. The little king looked very kind, thought he. I don't think he will turn me into a black stone. So he went to the priest, and the priest gave him some holy water as soon as he asked for it. Then Gluck took some bread in his basket, and the bottle of water, and set off very early for the mountains.

If the glacier had caused a great deal of fatigue in his brothers, it was twenty times worse for him, who was neither so strong nor so practised on the mountains. He had several very bad falls, lost his basket and bread, and was very much frightened at the strange noises under the ice. He lay a long time to rest on the grass and after he had recovered he began to climb the hill just in the hottest part of the day. When he had climbed for an hour, he got dreadfully thirsty, and was going to drink like his brothers, when he saw an old man coming down the path above him, looking very feeble, and leaning on a staff. 'My son,' said the old man, 'I am faint with thirst, give me some of that water.' Then Gluck looked at him, and when he saw that he was pale and weary, he gave him the water. 'Only pray don't drink it all,' said Gluck. But the old man drank a great deal, and gave him back the bottle two-thirds empty. Then he bade him good speed, and Gluck went on again merrily. And the path became easier to his feet, and two or three blades of grass appeared upon it, and some grass-hoppers began singing on the bank beside it, and Gluck thought he had never heard such merry singing.

Then he went on another hour, and the thirst increased on him so that he thought he should be forced to drink. But, as he raised the flask, he saw a little child lying panting by the roadside, and it cried out piteously for water. Then Gluck struggled with himself, and determined to bear the thirst a little longer; he put the bottle to the child's lips, and it drank all but a few drops. Then it smiled on him, and got up and ran down the hill. Gluck looked after it till it became as small as a little star, and then turned and began climbing again. And then there were all kinds of sweet flowers growing on the rocks, bright green moss, with pale pink starry flowers, and soft-belled gentians, more blue than the sky at its deepest, and pure white transparent lilies. And crimson and purple butterflies darted hither and thither, and the sky sent down such pure light that Gluck never felt so happy in his life.

Yet, when he had climbed for another hour, his thirst became intolerable again; and when he looked at his bottle, he saw that there were only five or six drops left in it, and he could not venture to drink. And as he was hanging the flask to his belt again, he saw a little dog lying on the rocks, gasping for breath – just as Hans had seen it on the day of his ascent. And Gluck stopped and looked at it, and then at the Golden River, not five hundred yards above him; and he thought of the dwarf's words, 'that no one could succeed, except in his first attempt'; and he tried to pass the dog, but it whined piteously, and Gluck stopped again. 'Poor beastie,' said Gluck, 'it'll be dead when I come down again, if I don't help it.' Then he looked closer and closer at it, and its eyes turned on him so mournfully, that he could not stand it. 'Confound the King and his gold too,' said Gluck; and he opened the flask, and poured all the water into the dog's mouth.

The dog sprang up and stood on its hind legs. Its tail disappeared, its ears became longer, silky and golden; its nose became very red, its eyes became very twinkling; in three seconds the dog was gone, and before Gluck stood his old acquaintance, the King of the Golden River.

'Thank you,' said the monarch, 'but don't be frightened, it's all right,' for Gluck looked stunned at this unlooked-for reply to his last remarks. 'Why didn't you come before,' continued the dwarf, 'instead of sending me those rascally brothers of yours, for me to have the trouble of turning into stones? Very hard stones they make too.'

'Oh dear me!' said Gluck, 'have you really been so cruel?'

'Cruel?' said the dwarf. 'They poured unholy water into my stream: do you suppose I'm going to allow that?'

'Why,' said Gluck, 'I am sure, sir – your majesty, I mean – they got the water out of the church font.'

'Very probably,' replied the dwarf; 'but', and his expression grew stern as he spoke, 'the water which had been refused to the cry of the weary and dying is unholy, even though it had been blessed by every saint in heaven; and the water which is found in the vessel of mercy is holy, even though it had been polluted with corpses.'

So saying, the dwarf stooped and plucked a lily that grew at his feet. On its white leaves there hung three drops of clear dew. And the dwarf shook them into the flask which Gluck held in his hand. 'Cast these into the river,' he said, 'and descend on the other side of the mountains into the Treasure Valley. And so good speed.'

As he spoke, the figure of the dwarf became indistinct. The playing colours of his robe formed themselves into a rainbow of dewy light: he stood for an instant veiled with them but slowly the colours grew faint, the mist rose into the air; the monarch had evaporated.

And Gluck climbed to the brink of the Golden River, and its waves were clear as crystal, and as brilliant as the sun. And, when he cast the three drops of dew into the stream, there opened where they fell a small circular whirlpool, into which the waters descended with a musical noise.

Gluck stood watching it for some time, very much disappointed, because not only the river was not turned into gold, but its waters seemed much less plentiful. Yet he obeyed his friend the dwarf, and descended the other side of the mountains, towards the Treasure Valley; and, as he went, he thought he heard the noise of water working its way under the ground. And, when he came in sight of the Treasure Valley, behold, a river, like the Golden River, was springing from a new cleft of the rocks above it, and was flowing in innumerable streams among the dry heaps of red sand.

And as Gluck gazed, fresh grass sprang beside the new streams, and creeping plants grew, and climbed among the moistening soil. Young flowers opened suddenly along the river sides, as stars leap out when twilight is deepening, and thickets of myrtle and tendrils of vine, cast lengthening shadows over the valley as they grew. And thus Treasure Valley became a garden again, and the rich lands which had been lost by cruelty, were regained by love.

And Gluck went, and dwelt in the valley, and the poor were never driven from his door, so that his barns became full of corn, and his house of treasure. And, for him, the river had, according to the dwarf's promise, become a River of Gold.

And to this day, the inhabitants of the valley point out the place where the three drops of holy dew were cast into the stream, and trace the course of the Golden River under the ground, until it emerges in Treasure Valley. And at the top of the cataract of the Golden River, are still to be seen two BLACK STONES, round which the waters howl mournfully every day at sunset.

The Rosy Apple and the Golden Bowl

There once lived an old man and woman and their three daughters. The two eldest daughters were vain and cruel, but the third, Tania, was quiet and modest in all she did. The eldest daughters were lazy and stupid and sat at home all day, but Tania busied herself in the house and garden from dawn to dusk. She would weed the vegetable bed, chop firewood, milk the cows and feed the chickens. Her sisters would make her do their chores for them, and she would go about her work without a word or a sigh.

One day the old man made ready to take some hay to market, promising to bring back gifts for each of his daughters.

The first daughter said:

'Buy me a length of blue silk, Father.'

The second daughter said:

'Buy me a length of red velvet.'

Tania said nothing.

The old man asked again.

'Come now, what shall I fetch you, my child?'

'Bring me a rosy apple and a golden bowl,' she said at last.

At that her sisters laughed so hard that they nearly split their sides.

'What a fool you are, Tanushka!' they cried. 'Why, we have a whole orchard of apples, you can pick as many as you please. And as for a bowl, why do you need that – to feed the ducks from?'

'No, dear sisters. I shall roll the apple in the bowl and say magic words. An old beggar once taught me them for giving her an Easter cake.'

Her sisters laughed even louder, and the old man reproached them:

'That's enough. I shall bring all of you the gifts you request.'

The old man sold his hay and bought his three daughters the gifts. For the first daughter he bought blue silk, for the second red velvet and for Tania a rosy apple and golden bowl.

The two eldest sisters were delighted with their gifts and at once set to making new dresses, all the while poking fun at their sister.

'Sit there and roll your apple, silly!' they called.

Tania sat quietly in a corner of the room rolling her rosy apple in the golden bowl, as she sang softly:

> Rosy apple, roll, roll
> Round my little golden bowl.
> Show me meadows and seas
> And forests and leas,
> And mountains so high
> They reach to the sky.

Suddenly bells began to ring and light flooded the whole cottage. Round and round the golden bowl rolled the rosy apple and, in the bowl as clear as day, there appeared:

> Downs and dales,
> Soldiers in fields with swords and shields,
> Grassy leas and ships on seas,
> And mountains so high they reached to the sky.

The two eldest sisters could hardly believe their eyes. Their only thought now was to find a way of taking the apple and bowl from their sister.

Tania, however, would not exchange her gift, never let the apple and bowl out of her sight and would play with them every evening.

One day, tired of waiting, the two sisters decided to lure her into the forest.

'Come, sweet sister,' they said, 'let us go and gather some berries

[28]

and flowers in the forest. We may find some wild strawberries for mother and father.'

In the forest there were no berries or flowers to be seen anywhere. Tania took out her golden bowl and rolled her rosy apple in it as she sang softly:

> Rosy apple, roll, roll
> Round the little golden bowl.
> Show me strawberry red and cornflower blue,
> Poppies and daisies and violets too.

At once the bells began to peal. Round and round the golden bowl rolled the rosy apple and, in the bowl, as clear as day, there appeared strawberry red and cornflower blue, poppies and daisies and violets too.

As Tania's two cruel sisters watched, a wicked gleam came into their eyes; while their sister sat quietly on a log staring down at her golden bowl, they killed her, buried her body beneath a silver birch and took the golden bowl and rosy apple for themselves. It was evening by the time they reached home, bringing baskets piled high with berries and flowers. They told their mother and father:

'Tania ran away from us and was lost. We searched the forest, but could not find her. The wolves or bears must have eaten her.'

On hearing that the mother burst into tears and the father said grimly:

'Roll the apple round the bowl and perhaps it will show us where Tania is.'

The sisters turned cold with fear, but they had to do as their father ordered. Yet when they tried to roll the apple in the bowl, it would not roll, and the bowl would not spin, and nothing appeared in it: no meadows or seas, no forests or leas, no mountains so high they reached to the sky.

Just about that time, a young shepherd was in the forest looking for a stray sheep and he came upon a silver birch with a fresh green mound beneath it and blue cornflowers growing around. Long slender reeds were shooting up amidst the flowers and from one of these the shepherd cut himself a pipe to play.

No sooner had he put the pipe to his lips than it began to play of itself. And these were the words it sang,

[29]

> Play, pipe, play, for the shepherd to hear,
> Play, pipe, play, for the shepherd to cheer.
> By my sisters I did die,
> Beneath the silver birch I lie.

The shepherd was frightened and ran straight to the village to tell his story. All the villagers gathered round to listen and gasped in horror.

When Tania's father heard the tale, he seized the pipe and put it to his own lips. The moment he did so it began to play by itself:

> Play, pipe, play, for my father to hear,
> Play, pipe, play, for my father to cheer.
> By my sisters I did die.
> Beneath the silver birch I lie.

The father put down the pipe and turned to the shepherd.

'Take me to where you cut the reed for your pipe,' he said.

The shepherd led him to the fresh green mound in the forest where cornflowers were growing beneath a silver birch tree. They dug a hole and found Tania in her shallow grave, quite cold and dead, but looking more lovely than ever, as if she were in peaceful slumber. And the pipe began to play again.

> Play, pipe, play, songs sad and gay,
> Listen, Father, to what I say:
> If you wish to see me well,
> Fetch some water from the royal well.

At these words, the two wicked sisters trembled and paled, fell on their knees and confessed their crime. The old man immediately set out for the king's palace to fetch the water.

When he finally reached the palace he was taken before the king.

The old man bowed to the ground and told his story. The king listened closely and said:

'You may take the water from my royal well and, if your daughter comes to life, bring her here together with her wicked sisters.'

The old man thanked the king and bowed low many times before going to the well and filling a flask with the water.

On returning to his dead daughter, he sprinkled her fair brow with the water from the royal well. Tania stirred, opened her eyes and embraced her parents.

The old man once more set off for the palace, this time with his three daughters; he arrived there and was again taken to the king. The king's gaze settled on Tania, as lovely as a spring flower, her eyes as radiant as the rays of the sun, her face as fair as the sky at dawn, and tears rolling down her cheeks like the purest of pearls.

'Where is your golden bowl and rosy apple?' the king said kindly.

As Tania took them out and spun the rosy apple round the golden bowl, there came a great ringing and pealing of bells and, one after the other, all the great Russian cities appeared in the bowl. Into the cities marched regiments of soldiers with their banners flying and their generals galloping ahead. Such was the firing and shooting, so thick the smoke that the battlefield was hidden from sight as if day had turned to night.

The rosy apple rolled on round the golden bowl and there appeared the sky in all its splendour: the bright sun chased away the pale crescent moon, fluffy white swans sailed in clouds across the sea-blue sky.

The king was filled with wonder at such marvellous sights, but Tania wept and wept without cease.

Finally, she went down on her knees before the king and begged:

'Please take my rosy apple and my golden bowl, Your Majesty. Only, pardon my sisters, do not put them to death because of me, I beg of you.'

The king gently lifted her to her feet and said:

'Your heart is of pure gold like your magic bowl. If you will consent to be my wife, you will not only make me happy but my people will have a kind and gentle queen. As for your sisters, they should be punished harshly, but, since you plead for their lives, I will spare them. Instead, they shall be banished to a bleak island at the other end of my kingdom.'

And so, the wicked sisters were banished and Tania became as noble a queen as the realm had seen.

Bertha Goldfoot

Bertha's father was a baron. He had a castle on the banks of the Rhine, or rather, on a rock above the bank; and under his castle on the edge of the water nestled the little village that paid him tribute, where the villagers led happy lives in their little houses with pointed red roofs, and in the vineyards on the hills between the village and the castle. For their baron was a fairly kind baron, which all the German barons in those times and parts were not.

It was the custom for every villager to bring the Baron a gold piece a year; and even in the hard years he could not let them off, because he himself had to pay tribute to the King. If he failed to do so the King might come down on him and seize his castle, and lands, and everything he had. And the villagers themselves would not have been so well off under anyone else as under their own baron; so they were as anxious as he was to keep the King in a good temper. Nobody had ever seen the King in those parts, but it was whispered that he only cared for money and dancing, and if he were denied them could show a very bad temper when he liked.

When Bertha was born, there was a christening, of course, and all the noblemen and noblewomen of the countryside came to it, and also, of course, all the chief fairies. The Baron and his wife tried to remember every fairy of importance, for they knew something bad might happen to their child if one was forgotten. They even invited the Lorelei, the lovely water nymph who sits and sings on a rock in the middle of the Rhine, and with her magic song draws men to their death. Many a friend of the Baron had been drowned at the foot of the Lorelei's rock, but the Baron did not dare leave her out, all the same. She did not appear, however, until the feast was over, and everybody had presented his gift and departed. Then, as the Baron and his wife and the baby's nurse were alone with little Bertha in her cradle, the doors of the great hall swung open, and the lovely Lorelei glided in, with her mantle of golden hair flowing about her like the golden waters of the Rhine. And, like the river, it was wet, and so were her green garments, and her white skin. She stepped up to the cradle, and leaning over touched the baby's right foot with her wet finger, saying,

'Child, men shall call you Bertha Goldfoot. The Lorelei gives you a foot of gold from the day you are able to walk.'

Then she glided out of the hall, leaving a trail of water on the floor behind her. And no one knew what she meant by her gift. While they were wondering, they heard a horrid little chuckle, and up through the floor popped Rumpelstiltskin, the Stocking-Elf. Everyone knows what a nasty little creature *he* is, and the Baron had not even thought of inviting him to the christening, because he is not of any great importance in the fairy world. Even if he was offended, it was not in his power to do very much harm, but they all felt uneasy as he hopped over to the cradle, and pointed his finger at Bertha's left foot.

'Child,' he croaked, 'you shall always have a hole in your left stocking as long as you live. That's what Rumpelstiltskin gives you for a christening-gift!'

With that he disappeared as suddenly as he had come. The Baron said, 'It's bad enough, but it might have been much worse.' And the Baron's wife said, 'For my part, I think the Lorelei's gift was the worse of the two. If the child grows up with a gold foot, how shall we ever get her married? Nobody would want a wife with such an oddity about her.'

'We must keep her foot covered up all the time, so that nobody shall guess,' said the Baron. 'See to it for us, Nanny,' he added, turning to her. 'Luckily the guests have all gone, and the three of us can keep Bertha's gold foot a secret between us until she is married.'

The first year of the baby's life, the nurse spent all her spare time in knitting stockings for Bertha, against the day when she would be able to walk; for it was then that she was to get her gold foot. The first time the nurse saw her totter on to her little feet, to try to run to her mother, she caught the child up, and pulled on her stockings, so that the whole of her feet and ankles were covered; for if a maid or a page had happened to catch a glimpse of the golden foot, the story would travel through the land. Then little Bertha was allowed to toddle as she pleased; but from that day she wore no more socks, because socks can slip down to the ankle.

Bertha even had to sleep in her stockings; and her nurse was careful always to change them at night in the dark, so that even she never saw Bertha's right foot after she was one year old. Her left foot, on the other hand, everybody saw; at least, they saw a part of it. For almost as soon as her left stocking was on, a big hole came in the heel like magic. It was no use scolding her, or watching to see how it happened – there the hole was! At first her nurse would change the stocking at once, but five minutes later she had to change it again, and at last she said to the Baron and his wife, 'It's no manner of good, my dears. We can't keep the holes from coming, so the child will have to wear boots.' And from the time she was about two, Bertha did. It wasn't very pleasant for her to have to wear boots from morning to night, no matter what she was doing, but it couldn't be helped. Boots she wore, from her babyhood to her eighteenth birthday, when she was as beautiful a young woman as any baron's daughter on the Rhine. Moreover, everybody loved her, from her parents to the barefoot boat-boy in the village, with whom she had often played in her childhood. As she grew older, suitors for her hand began to present themselves, but she cared for none of them.

Now this year was, as it happened, a terribly bad one for the vine harvest. The blight had got into it somehow; the grapes rotted, and the peasants in the village were as poor as church mice in consequence. At the end of the season they came weeping to the castle door and asked audience of the Baron.

'My lord,' said the chief vine-grower, 'our hearts are broken and our pockets too. We cannot pay you the tribute this year.'

'If you do not,' said the Baron, 'both you and I will be ruined. For the bad year has hit me as well as you, and if I do not pay him the King will descend on us in wrath.'

'My lord,' said the peasants, 'our children are starving, and we have nothing left. We would pay you gladly if we could; but who can pay what he has not got?'

The Baron was very angry, for he was not always a reasonable man; and kind as he really was, he was prepared to punish them, when Bertha, who was sitting at his feet, looked up at him saying, 'They cannot help it, Father. Let us hope for the best, and heaven will soften the King's heart or will send us the means to pay him.'

Her smile was so sweet that the Baron could not resist it, and he said to the peasant, 'Well, then, whatever bad fortune may fall upon us, we will share it together.' And the peasants returned to the village, thanking him and blessing his daughter.

But heaven did not soften the King's heart. He came riding in wrath, with his soldiers behind him, to demand the reason why the Baron had not paid him the tribute. The Baron pointed out to him the blighted vines, saying, 'There, sire, lies all my fortune, in ruins. The grapes were my gold and gave me the gold I gave you.'

'And gold I will have!' said the King. 'I care not for your reasons. If you cannot pay me, I will take your castle, your village, and all you possess.'

As he spoke, Bertha came into the hall. Her mother had dressed her in a gown of white silk, and crowned her head with her golden plaits, hoping that her beauty might win the King's heart, and save the day. Indeed, he stood amazed with admiration, and turning to the Baron said, 'Who is this maiden?'

'My daughter, sire,' he answered.

'In that case, Baron,' said the King, 'I will marry your daughter, and her wedding-portion shall be the debt you owe me.'

The Baron was overjoyed, and so was his wife. Bertha, poor child, turned as pale as her gown, and cast down her eyes before the King, who was admiring her from top to toe. But when his gaze *did* reach her toes, he frowned a little, and asked, 'Why does she wear boots?'

The Baron stammered hastily, 'She has been out walking, and has only just come in.'

'Put on your shoes,' said the King to Bertha, 'for I would like to see how my bride can dance.'

'I have no shoes, Your Majesty,' said Bertha; and this was true – she had never had a pair of shoes since she was a baby.

'Then I will dance with you in your stocking-feet,' said the King.

And it was no use protesting. Bertha had to take off her boots before him, and there, in the heel of her left stocking, was an enormous hole. The King looked surprised, and bade her go and change her stockings. But what was the use? She came back with a hole as big as before. A third time she tried, and still her rosy left heel was bare to everybody's view, and her cheeks were rosier still, as she hung her head and blushed for shame.

The King's admiration now turned to scorn, and he said to the Baron, 'Beautiful as your daughter is, I cannot have a slattern for my queen. Farewell; but if the money is not paid by tomorrow, I will turn you out of your castle.' So saying, he rode away.

The Baron now turned in anger on his daughter. 'It is you, with your wretched gift, who have brought me to this!' he cried. 'You are not fit to be my daughter, you slattern! Go away from my castle for ever, but go barefoot. It is better for the world to see your gold foot at last, than to see you with a hole in your stocking.'

He himself pulled off her stockings; and when he uncovered her right foot, lo and behold! it was as white as her left. What a surprise, for if Bertha's foot was not gold, what did the Lorelei mean by the gift? But the Baron was in too much of a rage to care about this; he lifted her in his arms and bore her down to the village, crying, 'My peasants, thanks to my daughter, I am now a beggar like yourselves. Who wants a beggar's daughter for his wife?'

While the people stood round amazed, the barefooted boat-boy, whom Bertha had played with as a child, stepped forward and said modestly, 'I want her, my lord, if she will have me.' And Bertha nodded her golden head, and the Baron, with a harsh laugh, gave her into the boy's arms and strode away. The boy called to the priest to ring the wedding bell at once, and set Bertha down on the ground; and for the first time since she was a year old, Bertha's bare foot touched the earth, and they walked to church together. But here is the strange thing. Wherever her right foot stepped, it left behind it a piece of gold. So that the whole of her way into church and out again was marked by a double line of shining coins. And the people following after cried in astonishment, 'Bertha Goldfoot! Look, there goes Bertha Goldfoot!' So it was for the rest of the day; the fiddler and piper struck up for the wedding dance, and the people danced in their shoes, with the barefoot bride and groom in their midst. And wherever Bertha danced, the gold danced under her very toes. By

midnight there was so much gold on the ground that the peasants were kept busy sweeping it up; and in the morning they carried it in a sack to the Baron and said, 'Here is our tribute, my lord. The village is saved.'

The Baron was now as joyful as he had been angry; he sent the gold post-haste to the King, and asked how it had all come about. And when he heard that it was all due to the wonderful gift of his own daughter, he hastened down to the village and forgave her.

'Come back to the castle with me, my darling child!' he said.

But Bertha shook her golden head and laughed. 'I cannot, Father. I am married now, and must live with my husband. Besides,' said she, 'I can never wear stockings again, for my gold foot loses its power unless it goes bare. But neither you nor the peasants need fear poverty any more.'

Her father embraced her, and saw that it must be so. And from then to the end of her days Bertha and her husband, and all their children too, lived barefoot.

Hercules and the Three Golden Apples of the Hesperides

Alcmene, granddaughter of Perseus, was the loveliest woman in all Greece. She was pledged in marriage to the good man Amphitryon and was eagerly awaiting his arrival in Thebes to celebrate their wedding.

Now Zeus, father of the immortal gods, was waiting for the hero to be born who would win great glory among men and who alone, it was prophesied, could save the gods from the Giants in the battles to come. This hero was to be born of mortal woman and yet to be the son of an immortal.

Zeus, therefore, plotted to marry Alcmene and to father her child. Disguised as Amphitryon, her husband-to-be, he flew down from Olympus and came to Alcmene in Thebes. She welcomed him, not suspecting who he really was and that night they were wedded. By his godly powers Zeus made that night the longest ever known to man. He commanded the moon to linger long in the skies and the sun to hold back his fiery chariot. Sleep stayed long with man so that the true Amphitryon was delayed and did not arrive at his bride's house till the next day, when Alcmene was wedded for the second time, only then learning of Zeus's deception.

The months passed till the day of the baby's birth. Zeus proudly spread the news amongst the immortals that a hero was to be born, destined one day to save them and be the mightiest hero of all Greece.

Hera, Zeus's goddess wife, was madly jealous of Alcmene and her child-to-be, who was the son of Zeus, and from that day she vowed she would give him no peace. She tricked Zeus into agreement that he, Heracles, as he was called (but known to the world as Hercules) when grown to manhood, should become the slave of his cousin, Eurystheus, who would, with Hera's help, send him on missions, any of which could mean almost certain and most horrible death. These missions became known as The Twelve Labours of Hercules.

The Babe Hercules and the Serpent

Hercules was born an hour before his twin brother, Iphicles (whose father was Amphitryon). He began to show his superhuman strength when still in his cradle. Alcmene had rocked her two little ones to sleep and as they slept two monstrous serpents came slithering along the ground hissing and spitting venom. Hera had sent them to destroy the babe Hercules, but when Alcmene and Amphitryon came rushing into the room in response to Iphicles's yells of terror, there was Hercules throttling a hissing snake in each of his tiny but power-ful hands. He then threw them dead on to the floor.

While still a youth Hercules killed a lion which attacked the cattle he was herding. He tracked the beast to its lair and was all but trapped as it leapt at him with its deadly claws, but Hercules was too quick and dealt it a mighty blow with his club. Twice he struck the lion and twice the beast returned to the fray, but a third blow finished it off and Hercules flung the lion skin over his shoulders as armour for his body, while the head he used as a protective helmet.

Now Hercules had grown to manhood but still Hera had not had her revenge, so she cursed him with a plague of madness which caused him unknowingly to kill his own children whom he loved most dearly. To be cured of his madness Hercules was told he must go to Delphi to ask Apollo how he must atone for the terrible deed.

'Hercules, son of Zeus,' came the voice of the oracle, 'the time has come for you to carry out the superhuman tasks to be imposed on you by your cousin, Eurystheus, King of Mycenae, and you will perform them, however daunting, and these labours will make you famed as the greatest hero ever known. And it shall be that one day you will win from Zeus a place among the immortals.'

So Hercules, wrapped in his lion skin, came to Eurystheus in his citadel at Tiryns.

The Labours of Hercules

Now the cruel and cowardly Eurystheus was gleeful at the thought that the kind of labours he would impose on Hercules would mean his certain death.

But Hercules strangled *with his bare hands* the ferocious Nemean lion who was utterly invulnerable to any weapons known to man. Carrying the carcass of the fearsome beast, Hercules returned to his task-master, his FIRST LABOUR performed. Eurystheus recoiled in terror at the sight of the dead lion, with Hercules himself safe and sound.

Hercules performed many more impossible feats. He decapitated the nine-headed Lernean Hydra, a poisonous water-snake whose very breath was so foul as to prove fatal to anyone who ventured close enough. The monster sprouted two heads from each beheaded neck, so Hercules singed each neck-end till the last head was struck off and this he buried under a gigantic rock.

His SECOND LABOUR done, Eurystheus sent him on his THIRD and Hercules returned bringing back the Erymanthian Boar alive, but Eurystheus was so terrified at the sight of it, even though its legs were tied, that he jumped into a huge brass jar and remained hidden till Hercules had removed the Boar and flung it into the sea.

Yet another Labour was for Hercules to cleanse, in one day, the Augean Stables, which contained the dung of three thousand oxen and no one had dared clean them for thirty years. This Hercules achieved by diverting the paths of two mighty rivers.

He chased the terrifying Stymphalian Birds away and yet another Labour was to bring back the mad Cretan Bull, which once again sent the cowardly Eurystheus with a leap of terror into his brass pot where he stayed till he learnt the bull had escaped. In yet a further task Hercules brought back to his master the fierce horses of King Diomedes which had never before been bridled.

From the Amazon Queen Hippolyta Hercules secured the famous Girdle which Eurystheus demanded for his sister.

In the performance of his Labours Hercules met with many strange adventures. His rescue of the beauteous Alcestis and his almighty struggle with Death, who had claimed her as his rightful victim, was the most wondrous of them all.

Now, when Hercules drove the cattle of the three-headed giant Geryon (who had six arms and was said to be the strongest man in the world) back to his master, he cried triumphantly, 'I have now performed the ten labours you have set me, so now you must let me go free.'

'Not so fast,' mocked Eurystheus, 'You cheated in two of your labours, so Hera commands that you do two further tasks.'

So the mighty hero had to submit and his ELEVENTH LABOUR was to bring back:

Three Golden Apples from the Garden of the Hesperides

The Golden Apples had been given to Hera as a wedding present and were in the keeping of the daughters of Hesperis. But Hercules had no idea where the Golden Apples were and after searching far and wide he consulted the Old Man of the Sea, Nereus, who alone knew their secret hiding place. Hercules tried to force him to reveal his secret, but all he would tell him was that he must ask the Nymphs of Illyria. They in turn told him that by the command of Father Zeus, he must travel to Mount Caucasus and ask the Titan Prometheus where they were. Prometheus had been punished for stealing the heavenly fire from the gods and presenting it to mankind. Zeus had had him chained to the Caucasus rocks. Every day a great eagle came and tore out his liver and every night it grew again.

Now Prometheus knew many things. He had prophesied the birth of Hercules and knew, too, of a great danger that was threatening Zeus, but still he refused to tell Zeus what that danger was, so still he remained chained. But now Zeus's heart was softened. Prometheus had sacrificed himself enough and suffered nobly. And Hercules was sent to free him.

High upon the cliff edge the heroic Titan was tied in chains to the rocks and Hercules heard his cries of agony as the voracious eagle swooped down upon his prey. But Hercules drew his bow and let fly an arrow that caught the bird in mid-flight. The great bird plummeted to the swirling seas below. 'By the command of Zeus my father,' cried Hercules, 'I have come to set you free. Too long have you been tortured for your disobedience to him and he begs your forgiveness.' Then he proceeded to cut the fetters that enchained the Titan and that day was he freed.

Then Prometheus told Hercules where he must go for the Golden Apples. 'They are to be found on the tree which Mother Earth gave to Hera on her wedding day. The tree itself is in an enchanted garden on the western edge of the earth. You must first journey to the world's highest mountain on top of which stands Atlas, my brother Titan, holding up the heavens. It is he who will assist you.'

So Hercules went on his way, deeply humbled at the thought of the noble Titan, who had endured so much to help mankind.

On this hazardous journey to seek out Atlas, Hercules had first to get past the giant son of Earth, Antaeus, who challenged all strangers to wrestle with him. Hercules was only too glad to accept the challenge. Exploiting his very superior strength it was not long before he had flung his opponent to the ground. But then, amazingly, Antaeus sprang to his feet again, stronger and more vigorous than before, his secret being that as soon as he touched the Earth (his mother), all weakness passed from him and left him more powerful than before the contest began. And this happened many times until the truth dawned on Hercules. So instead of hurling Antaeus to the ground, he summoned all his mighty strength and hoisted him up and held him aloft until he grew so weak that Hercules was able to squeeze the very life out of him. Then he flung aside the corpse and continued his journey to the world's highest mountain on the top of which Atlas held up the heavens.

'I am Hercules, son of Zeus,' he said, 'and your Titan brother, Prometheus, told me to seek your help. I come for the Three Golden Apples from the Garden of the Hesperides, which I must deliver to Eurystheus, my master.' 'I will myself gladly get the apples,' replied Atlas, 'for no mortal man may enter the garden. But first you must slay the dragon, Ladon, who is coiled round the foot of the tree. For while he is alive, I may not touch the fruit of that tree. And, of course, while I am away, you must support the heavens on your shoulders.'

Beyond the mountain to the west Hercules could see the shining

[43]

gold scales of the dragon at the bottom of the tree on which the Golden Apples grew, while the three daughters of Hesperis danced and sang around it. Hercules fitted an arrow to his bow and with unerring aim let it fly at the dragon's throat. The beast slowly uncurled itself from the tree and glided sinuously to the nearby bushes, there to die slowly – so slowly indeed that years later, when the Argonauts, Hercules among them, passed this way on their Quest for the Golden Fleece, the dragon's tail was still seen writhing and lashing in its death agony.

Then Atlas, with a mighty sigh of relief, shifted the sky on to Hercules's massive shoulders and sped to the garden. Throughout the night Hercules held his heavy burden and in the morning he was relieved to see Atlas coming up the mountain bearing the Golden Apples in his hand. But crafty Atlas paused some distance away with a glint of mischievous triumph in his eyes.

'Listen, Hercules,' he said, 'I will myself take these apples to Eurystheus while you keep holding up the sky.'

But Hercules, no less wily than Atlas and pretending to agree with him, requested him to hold the skies for a mere minute whilst he would arrange a sort of pad for the convenience of his shoulders. And while the change was being made, Hercules picked up the Apples and hastened away to Eurystheus, leaving Atlas dismayed at losing his one and only chance of ever regaining his freedom.

When Hercules delivered the Apples, Eurystheus no longer wanted them, so Hercules handed them to Aphrodite to be returned to the Garden of the Hesperides. It was then that she took pity on Atlas still holding up the skies; she showed him the Gorgon's head which turned him to stone. Thus Atlas turned into what became known as the topmost peak of Mount Atlas.

Hercules had performed his ELEVENTH LABOUR. But now came from Eurystheus the most dreaded command ever given by man to man. Hercules must descend to Hades, the Land of the Dead, and bring back Cerberus, the three-headed Hound of Hell.

For this Hercules must cross the River Styx where Charon, the old Ferryman, was allowed only to ferry dead souls, and then he must capture the beast without the use of any weapon. The hound's three heads were covered with manes bristling with writhing snakes lashing out in all directions.

Then Hercules, knowing that he was aided by the all-powerful

Zeus, stepped into Charon's boat and demanded that he be ferried across. He had directed a glower of such ferocity at the Ferryman that, even though well aware of the due punishment he must suffer – Hercules being no corpse! – Charon still transported him across the deadly River Styx right to the portals of the Underworld.

Here he met his dreaded adversary. Hercules then wrapped his lion skin round his body, seized the monstrous Cerberus round the middle and squeezed him tighter and tighter till the wretched dog gave up the struggle. Only when Hercules presented him to Eurystheus did he howl and hiss from his besnaked heads.

But Eurystheus had leapt into his brass pot in terror and yelled from within: 'Take the monster back to Hades. You have performed your TWELVE LABOURS with unflinching courage. You are now free.'

And Hercules rejoiced.

Greed for Gold

All over the world there are people who give up worldly things and spend much time in prayer and meditation. This is a story from India about such a holy man – a sadhu – who tried to help three people . . . but people don't always listen to good advice.

A holy man was once walking alone in a desert. His eyes were fixed on the ground as he prayed silently. Rocks and boulders were all around but nothing grew. Nothing seemed to move in this barren place except the holy man. There were no animals or birds about. Even the lizards and small insects had crawled under the rocks to hide from the sun's fierce rays.

Looking for shade, the holy man came across a narrow opening in the rocks. He peered in and found a small cave. 'Perhaps I can rest here in the shade, away from the cruel sun,' he said to himself. And he crept through the opening. Inside, it was cool and dark – such a change from the burning glare outside. Sighing with relief, he stretched out in a corner and looked around him. One corner of the cave was unusually bright.

'How strange!' he said; and he moved closer. One weak ray of sun had filtered through the narrow cave opening and reached this spot. Now it was reflected many times amongst a heap of . . . gold!

As soon as he realized what lay there before him in a glittering, tempting pile, the holy man jumped up and ran out of the cave as fast as he could.

Now it so happened that three thieves had chosen to hide in this part of the desert. And that day, as usual, they lay in wait behind a large rock – ready to jump out and rob lonely travellers.

It wasn't long before the holy man came running towards them. He stopped, from time to time, to peer over his shoulder and the thieves watched him closely. Then they looked at each other in alarm. The road was empty. There was no one chasing him. . . .

'What is the *sadhu* – the holy man – running from?' they wondered. They stepped from their hiding place and the holy man blundered straight into them. He couldn't stop running and the three thieves had to hold him fast to steady him.

'Peace be to you, *sadhu*, what troubles you?' they asked politely, placing their palms together as a sign of respect.

'Brothers,' he gasped, 'I am running from the Devil. The Devil is after me!' And he looked behind him, his face full of terror. He tried to run but the thieves held him firmly. They were puzzled. They felt that a holy man like the *sadhu* would not lie to them and yet they could see nobody on the long, lonely road.

'The Devil?' they asked. 'We see nothing. Come, holy man. Show us what is after you.'

The holy man was silent.

'Don't be afraid, *sadhu*. We won't hurt you,' the thieves said, 'but we won't let you go until you show us.'

At last the holy man agreed. 'If that is your desire,' he said, 'then let it be so.' And he led them to the cave. But he stopped outside it.

'Brothers,' he said, 'I beg you, don't go in! Take an old man's advice. Leave things as they are for Evil lies within.'

By this time the thieves were very curious. What was the cause of the old man's alarm? And they insisted on entering the cave. Although it was dark inside, they were immediately drawn to the bright corner. When they saw the gold, they were astonished. They fell on their knees and began to count the pieces.

'Brothers, beware,' warned the holy man, pointing to the glittering heap. 'Do not be tempted. Here lies Death. It was Death who sent the Devil to tempt me. And I ran away from them . . . from the Devil and Death!'

The thieves took no notice of what the old man was saying. They were too busy, greedily running their hands through the piles of gold.

'Run, brothers! Run away from the Devil and Death!' the holy man pleaded.

The thieves looked at each other, then shrugged their shoulders.

'The holy man's crazy,' one said.

'Too much walking about in the sun!' said another, whilst the third took the tired old man out of the cave and sent him on his way.

The thieves could hardly believe their good fortune. What would they do with all that gold? Share it equally amongst themselves, they decided. But there was so much to be shared out. It would take a long time and they were hungry. They could not leave the gold unattended so one of them volunteered to take some of it to buy food. As soon as he returned, they would share the rest of the gold between them.

When he arrived in town, the thief said to himself, 'I will eat here alone. Then I will poison the food I take back so that it kills those two in the cave. In that way, *all* the treasure will be mine!'

While he was away, his two friends in the cave plotted.

'As soon as he comes here,' they said, 'we will kill him. Then, after we have eaten, we will divide all this gold between just the *two* of us.'

As soon as the thief returned to the cave with the provisions, his two friends killed him. Then they sat down to feast on the food he had brought. Within an hour, both of them fell dead – poisoned by the food their friend had prepared for them. Around them lay the scattered treasure, still glittering in the cave. 'Run, brothers! Run away from the Devil and Death,' the holy man had begged them. But they had ignored his warning. Their greed for the gold had been too great. And, in the end, the holy man's prediction had come true . . . 'Here lies Death'.

The Yellow Dwarf and the
King of the Golden Mines

Once upon a time there was a Queen who had an only daughter, and she was so fond of her that she never corrected her faults; therefore the Princess became so proud, and so vain of her beauty that she despised everybody. The Queen gave her the name of Toutebelle; and sent her portrait to several friendly kings. As soon as they saw it, they all fell in love with her. The Queen, however, saw no means of inducing her to decide in favour of one of them, so, not knowing what to do, she went to consult a powerful Fairy, called the Fairy of the Desert: but it was not easy to see her, for she was guarded by lions. The Queen would have had little chance if she had not known how to prepare a cake that would appease them. She made one herself, put it into a little basket, and set out on her journey.

Being tired with walking, she lay down at the foot of a tree and fell asleep; and on awaking, she found her basket empty, and the cake gone, while the lions were roaring dreadfully. 'Alas, what will become of me!' she exclaimed, clinging to the tree. Just then she heard, 'Hist! A-hem!' and raising her eyes, she saw up in the tree a little man not more than two feet high. He was eating oranges, and said to her, 'I know you well, Queen; you have good reason to be afraid of the lions, for they have devoured many before you, and – you have no cake.'

'Alas,' cried the poor Queen, 'I should die with less pain if my dear daughter were but married!'

'How! you have a daughter!' exclaimed the yellow Dwarf. (He was so called from the colour of his skin, and his living in an orange tree.) 'I am delighted to hear it, for I have sought a wife by land and sea. If you will promise her to me, I will save you from the lions.'

The Queen looked at him, and was scarcely less frightened at his horrible figure than at the lions. She made no answer until she saw them on the brow of a hill, running towards her. At this the poor Queen cried out, 'Save me! Toutebelle is yours.' The trunk of the orange tree immediately opened: the Queen rushed into it; it closed, and the lions were baulked of their prey.

The unfortunate Queen then dropped insensible to the ground, and while she was in this state she was transported to the palace, and placed in her own bed. When she awoke and recollected what had befallen her, she tried to persuade herself that it was all a dream and that she had never met with this dreadful adventure: but she fell into a melancholy state, so that she could scarcely speak, eat, or sleep.

The Princess, who loved her mother with all her heart, grew very uneasy. She often begged her to say what was the matter, but the Queen always put her off with some reason that the Princess saw plainly enough was not the real one. Being unable to control her anxiety, she resolved to seek the famous Fairy of the Desert, whose advice as to marrying she was also desirous of obtaining, for everybody pressed her to choose a husband. She took care to knead the cake herself, and pretending to go to bed early one evening, she went out by a back staircase, and thus, all alone, set out to find the Fairy. But on arriving at the orange tree, she was seized with a desire to gather some of the fruit. She set down her basket and plucked some oranges; but when she looked again for it, it had disappeared. Alarmed and distressed, she suddenly saw beside her the frightful little Dwarf.

'What ails you, fair maid?' said he.

'Alas!' replied she, 'I have lost the cake which was so necessary to ensure my safe arrival at the abode of the Desert Fairy.'

'And what do you want with her?' said the Dwarf. 'I am her kinsman, and as clever as she is.'

'The Queen, my mother,' replied the Princess, 'has lately fallen into despair. I fancy I am the cause of it, for she wishes me to marry; but I

[51]

have not yet seen any one I think worthy of me. It is for this reason I would consult the Fairy.'

'Don't give yourself that trouble, Princess,' said the Dwarf; 'I can advise you better than she. The Queen is sorry that she has promised you in marriage.'

'The Queen promised me!' cried the Princess. 'Oh, you must be mistaken.'

'Beautiful Princess,' said the Dwarf, flinging himself at her feet, 'it is I who am destined to enjoy such happiness.'

'My mother have you for her son-in-law!' exclaimed Toutebelle, recoiling; 'was there ever such madness!'

'I care very little about the honour,' said the Dwarf, angrily. 'Here come the lions; in three bites they will avenge me.' At the same moment the poor Princess heard the roars of the savage beasts.

'What will become of me?' she cried. The Dwarf looked at her, and laughed contemptuously.

'Be not angry,' said the Princess; 'I would rather marry all the dwarfs in the world than perish in so frightful a manner.'

'Look at me well, Princess, before you give me your word,' replied he.

'I have looked at you more than enough,' said she. 'The lions are approaching; save me!' She had scarcely uttered these words, when she fainted.

On recovering, she found herself in her own bed, and on her finger a little ring made of a single red hair, which fitted her so closely that the skin might have been taken off sooner than the ring. When the Princess saw these things, and remembered what had taken place, she became very despondent, which pained the whole Court.

Toutebelle had now lost much of her pride. She saw no better way of getting out of her trouble than by marrying some great king with whom the Dwarf would not dare to dispute. She therefore consented to marry the King of the Golden Mines, a very powerful and handsome Prince, who loved her passionately. It is easy to imagine his joy when he received this news. Everything was prepared for one of the grandest entertainments that had ever been given. The King of the Golden Mines sent home for such sums of money that the sea was covered with the ships which brought them. Now that she had accepted him, the Princess found in the young King so much merit that she soon began to return his affection, and became very warmly attached to him.

At length the day so long wished for arrived. Everything being ready for the marriage, the people flocked in crowds to the great square in front of the palace. The Queen and Princess were advancing to meet the King, when they saw two large turkey-cocks, drawing a strange-looking box. Behind them came a tall old woman, whose age and decrepitude were no less remarkable than her ugliness. She leaned on a crutch. She wore a black ruff, a red hood, and a gown all in tatters. She took three turns round the gallery with her turkey-cocks before she spoke a word; then, stopping and brandishing her crutch, she cried, 'Ho! ho! Queen – Ho! ho! Princess! Do you fancy you can break your promises to my friend the Yellow Dwarf! I am the Fairy of the Desert! But for him and his orange tree, know you not that my great lions would have devoured you?'

'Ah! Princess,' exclaimed the Queen bursting into tears, 'what promise have you made?'

'Ah! Mother,' cried Toutebelle, sorrowfully, 'what promise have *you* made?'

The King of the Golden Mines, enraged at this interruption, advanced upon the old woman, sword in hand, and cried, 'Quit this palace for ever, or with thy life thou shalt atone for thy malice!'

Scarcely had he said this when the lid of the box flew up as high as the ceiling, with a terrific noise, and out of it issued the Yellow Dwarf, mounted on a large Spanish cat, who placed himself between the Fairy of the Desert and the King of the Golden Mines. 'Rash youth!' cried he, 'think not of assaulting this illustrious Fairy: it is with me alone thou hast to do! The faithless Princess who would give thee her hand has plighted her troth to me, and received mine. Look if she have not on her finger a ring of my hair.'

'Miserable monster,' said the King to him, 'hast thou the audacity to declare thyself the lover of this divine Princess?'

The Yellow Dwarf struck his spurs into the sides of his cat, which set up a terrific squalling and frightened everybody but the King, who pressed the Dwarf so closely that he drew a cutlass, and defying him to single combat, descended into the courtyard, the enraged King following him. Scarcely had they confronted each other, the whole Court being in the balconies to witness the combat, when the sun became as red as blood, and it grew so dark that they could scarcely see themselves. The two turkey-cocks appeared at the side of the Yellow Dwarf, casting out flames from their mouths and eyes. All

these horrors did not shake the heart of the young King; but his courage failed when he saw the Fairy of the Desert, mounted upon a winged griffin and armed with a lance, rush upon his dear Princess and strike so fierce a blow that she fell into the Queen's arms bathed in her own blood. The King ran to rescue the Princess, but the Yellow Dwarf was too quick for him; he leaped with his cat into the balcony, snatched the Princess from the arms of the Queen, and disappeared with her.

The King was gazing in despair on this extraordinary scene, when he felt his eyesight fail; and by some irresistible power he was hurried through the air. The wicked Fairy of the Desert had no sooner set her eyes on him than her heart was touched by his charms. She bore him off to a cavern, where she loaded him with chains; and she hoped that the fear of death would make him forget Toutebelle.

As soon as they had arrived there, she restored his sight, and appeared before him like a lovely nymph. 'Can it be you, charming Prince?' she cried. 'What misfortune has befallen you?'

The King replied, 'Alas, fair nymph, I know not the object of the unkind Fairy who brought me hither.'

'Ah, my Lord,' exclaimed the nymph, 'if you are in the power of that woman you will not escape without marrying her.' Whilst she thus pretended to take great interest in the King's affliction, he caught sight of her feet, which were like those of a griffin, and by this at once knew her to be the wicked Fairy. He, however, took no notice of it.

'I do not', said he, 'entertain any dislike to the Fairy of the Desert, but I cannot endure that she should keep me in chains like a criminal.'

The Fairy of the Desert, deceived by these words, resolved to carry the King to a beautiful spot. So she made him enter her chariot, to which she had now harnessed swans, and fled with him from one pole to the other.

Whilst thus travelling through the air, he beheld his dear Princess in a castle all of steel, the walls of which, reflecting the rays of the sun, became like burning-glasses, and scorched to death all who ventured to approach them. She was reclining on the bank of a stream. As she lifted her eyes, she saw the King pass by with the Fairy of the Desert, who, through her magic arts, seemed to be very beautiful; and this made her more unhappy than ever, as she thought the King was untrue to her. She thus became jealous, and was offended with the poor King, while he was in great grief at being so rapidly borne away from her.

At length they reached a meadow, covered with a thousand various flowers. A deep river surrounded it, and in the distance arose a superb palace. As soon as the swans had descended, the Fairy of the Desert led the King into a handsome apartment, and did all she could that he might not think himself actually a prisoner.

The King, who had his reasons for saying kind things to the old Fairy, was not sparing of them, and by degrees obtained leave to walk by the seaside. One day he heard a voice, and looking rapidly around him, he saw a female of great beauty, whose form terminated in a long fish's tail. As soon as she was near enough to speak to him, she said, 'I know the sad state to which you are reduced by the loss of your Princess; if you are willing, I will convey you from this fatal spot.' As the King hesitated, the Siren said, 'Do not think I am laying a snare for you; if you will confide in me, I will save you.'

'I have such perfect confidence in you,' said the King, 'that I will do whatever you command.'

'Come with me then,' said the Siren; 'I will first leave on the shore a figure so perfectly resembling you that it shall deceive the Fairy, and then convey you to the Steel Castle.'

She cut some sea-rushes, and making a large bundle of them, they became so like the King of the Golden Mines that he had never seen so astonishing a change. The friendly Siren then made the King seat himself upon her great fish's tail, and carried him off.

They soon arrived at the Steel Castle. The side that faced the sea was the only part of it that the Yellow Dwarf had left open. The Siren told the King that he would find Toutebelle by the stream near which he had seen her when he passed over with the Fairy. But as he would have to contend with some enemies before he could reach her, she gave him a diamond sword, with which he could face the greatest danger, warning him *never to let it fall*. The King thanked the Siren warmly, and strode on rapidly towards the Steel Castle.

Before he had gone far four terrible sphinxes surrounded him, and would quickly have torn him in pieces, if the diamond sword had not proved as useful to him as the Siren had predicted. He dealt each of them its death-blow, then advancing again, he met six dragons, covered with scales. But his courage remained unshaken and, making good use of his sword, there was not one that he did not cut in half at

[56]

a blow. Without further obstacle, he entered the grove in which he had seen Toutebelle. She was seated beside the fountain, pale and suffering. At first she indignantly fled from him.

'Do not condemn me unheard,' said he. 'I am an unhappy lover, who has been compelled, despite himself, to offend you.' He flung himself at her feet, but in so doing he unfortunately let fall the sword. The Yellow Dwarf, who had lain hidden behind a shrub, no sooner saw it out of the King's hands than he sprang forward to seize it. The Princess uttered a loud shriek, which luckily caused the King to turn suddenly round, just in time to snatch up the sword. With one blow he slew the wicked Dwarf, and then conducted the Princess to the seashore, where the friendly Siren was waiting to convey them to the Queen. On their arrival at the palace, the wedding took place, and Toutebelle, cured of her vanity, lived happily with the King of the Golden Mines.

Midas and the Golden Touch

In the time of the ancient Greeks King Midas ruled over the land of Phrygia. He was a good king and the people loved him.

Midas's palace was famed for its riches and more especially for its rose gardens. Visitors would come from far and wide to catch a glimpse of the splendid blooms and delicate hues and to breathe their fragrant scents.

Since Midas was exceedingly rich, his palace was naturally of the utmost splendour. Its pillars were golden and its lavish furnishings were all inlaid with gold. His tableware and drinking cups were of gold and even his singing bird lived in an elaborate golden cage. The throne from which he gave his royal commands was of solid gold. His robes were of the finest cloth, spun from shimmering gold thread. His golden carriage was so grand that people lined the streets to gaze upon it open-mouthed as he rode forth each morning from the palace.

Midas loved gold. It was his one weakness. His desire for it grew stronger from day to day till it all but took possession of him. He wanted more gold, and more, and more, and still more.

He began to spend most of his time in his treasure vaults, counting the precious coins and lovingly fingering the golden jewellery, all the while gazing in an ecstasy of pleasure at all his other precious gems – the rubies, the amethysts, the sapphires and emeralds which filled his vast chests to overbrimming. He even took to locking himself in, alone and uninterrupted, under the spell of these gleaming possessions as they glittered in the sunlight peeping through the narrow chinks of his vaults.

King Midas had a little daughter whom he loved more than anything in the world. Her golden tresses fell round her pretty little face, and an entracing picture she made as she frolicked merrily round her father's throne or skipped alongside him as he strolled through the palace gardens with their profusion of roses. She thought they were the loveliest flowers in the world when he picked her up for her to breathe her full share of their scent. And she would dance and sing as they made their way by the stream that flowed through the rose gardens.

One morning the gardeners came across an old man asleep in a drunken stupor on the grass. They bound him with garlands of flowers and carried him to the king. Midas at once recognized his prisoner – none other than the jolly Silenus, rubicund and rotund. He had been tutor to the god Dionysus, the god of wine; Silenus was one of his faithful band of followers and his very dear friend. Midas, too, was a great admirer of Dionysus and was honoured to have a friend of his in his palace. He invited Silenus to be his guest, and for ten days he wined and dined and entertained him with all manner of delightful amusements. And during this time Silenus told his host all manner of tales of wondrous lands far away across the seas. And Midas was enchanted.

At the end of that time Silenus was escorted back to Dionysus, whose followers had been searching everywhere for him. So pleased was Dionysus to find his lost companion that he sent a messenger to Midas indicating that he would grant him any reward he chose to name. 'The god Dionysus', the messenger announced, 'bade me warn you to make your wish wisely and to think carefully before you do so. What, then, King Midas, shall I tell the god is your dearest wish?'

Midas thought and thought, but his every thought could turn on only one thing and one thing only – GOLD. If he could *make* gold, he could have veritable mountains of it, reaching up to the skies. So, boldly, without further hesitation, he proclaimed his most heartfelt desire. 'Tell the great Dionysus that Midas wishes to possess the Golden Touch, so that anything he touches will turn to gold. If this wish is fulfilled he will be the happiest man in the world.'

When Dionysus heard this wish he sighed, but nevertheless he kept his promise. He dispatched his messenger back to King Midas with these words, 'Tomorrow at sunrise you will find yourself endowed with the Golden Touch.'

Hardly had night given way to dawn when Midas, who had not slept a wink all night, decided to test Dionysus's promised gift. He stretched out his eager hand and touched everything in reach that wasn't already gold – a chair, a flower vase, a silken cushion – but was bitterly disappointed to find that they remained completely unchanged. He lay back on his bed, as miserable as though he had been the poorest man in the world. He had worked himself up to such a pitch of excited expectation that he felt he could not live if this Golden Touch were denied him. He gazed gloomily out at the grey skies . . . then, suddenly, he sprang up in stunned amazement. With the first rays of the rising sun the bed covers he was touching had been transformed into a texture of the purest gold. As he drew back the curtains around his bed, he saw that they too had been transmuted into gold.

In a frenzy of excitement Midas rushed down the carpeted staircase, each step as he trod on it changing into the coveted metal. The banister, as his hand skimmed it, became a bar of burnished gold.

Then out into the palace grounds – he couldn't wait to see a forest of golden trees – and next to his roses, his exquisite roses. With one feather touch each bloom hardened into a golden rose, its delicate petals inclining to the gilded stem. Even the veins on the leaves stood out boldly in golden relief. He plucked an apple from a golden branch and gazed in wonder at its little gold stalk as he felt the golden roundness of it in his palm.

He walked with silent bliss up the now golden steps to his palace, turning walls, corridors and alcoves to the metal of his desire. But he was ready now to eat a hearty breakfast. He sat down at the table to await, as usual, the arrival of his little daughter. To his great surprise, however, and as an unpleasant awakening from his day-dream, he was distressed to see her looking more miserable than he had ever seen her and actually crying. Midas, thinking to cheer her up, leaned across the table to touch her little bowl and transform it into glistening gold. Now this bowl was much loved by his daughter, for its quaint little figures and pretty flowers arranged around the top rim gave her great delight to pore over when she had finished her food. 'But when it is golden,' thought Midas, 'she will love it even more.'

'What is it, my dear daughter, that saddens you and makes you sob so piteously?' he asked. She held out one of the roses which Midas had so recently changed to gold. 'It's horrid, it's hard and ugly,' she sobbed. 'I can't smell its lovely scent. I ran out into the garden to gather a sweet bunch of roses for you – I know how much you love them – but they had all turned this nasty yellow colour and they are no longer soft and velvety. What's happened to our roses? Where's their perfume gone?'

Midas tried hard to comfort his little daughter. 'Eat your breakfast, my dear, and afterwards I shall explain it all to you and you will be the happiest little girl in the world.'

Midas reached out for a piece of bread, but before he had broken it, it had changed to gold and the hard metal jarred his teeth. He raised his goblet to sip a little wine, but his delight at feeling the goblet turn to gold was instantly destroyed when unpleasant molten gold touched his lips. He transferred some meat to his plate with his fork, thinking that the fork would come between his teeth and the food, but again he found his teeth meeting the hard metal. His throat was parched with thirst and he was feeling very hungry indeed. 'I shall die of starvation,' he thought with terror. In desperation he grabbed at a large plum, stuffing it into his mouth, stone and all, thinking that speed would be the answer to his Golden Touch – beating it at its own game. But to no avail. Before a single drop of its delicious juice could ooze on to his palate, the plum was as hard as the metal it had now changed into.

Such a sumptuously appetizing breakfast-table – a table groaning with the choicest meats and fruits, bread, wine and sweetmeats – and not one single thing could he eat or drink. The poor man was terrified. What would become of him? Here he was with the gift that would make him the richest king in the world, yet not a bite to be eaten or a drop to be drunk. He would surely die.

He looked helplessly at his little daughter, who had just finished her food and was staring in dismay at her bowl, whose pretty figures stared metallically back at her. But as she waited for her father to

explain it all, the little girl could see that he was in a state of extreme distress. It dawned on her that something dreadful had happened.

'Father, dearest father,' she cried, running up to him, 'what is it? What is the matter?' She threw her arms around his neck while he hugged and kissed her. At that moment he felt that his daughter's love was worth infinitely more than the Golden Touch. 'My little one!' he cried. But the little one made no response, nor did she stir. Nor could she. For the moment she had flung herself into his arms and his lips had touched her forehead she had become a cold, gold statue. Her golden curls now hung stiffly round her little golden face. The tears on her cheeks had congealed. He held her in his arms but her little body was no longer soft.

Midas raised his arms in horror and cried out in agony to the gods, begging forgiveness for his stupid greed for gold.

The god Dionysus heard Midas's cry of despair and could not refrain from mocking him for the folly of his wish. Yet he did feel sympathy for the mortal who would now gladly have forfeited every grain of gold in the world if he could only have restored the cold gold little figure in his arms to her soft warm self.

So once more Dionysus sent down his messenger to the king. 'Oh, rid me of this accursed gift!' cried Midas in anguish as soon as he appeared, tearing in frenzy at the roots of his hair – which, of course, stiffened as he did so. 'Pray tell the great Dionysus that I rue to the very depths of my being the arrant stupidity of my wish and repent the choice that I so greedily made. I have lost that which means more to me than anything in this life. If he will deign to help me regain my normal mortal powers, never again will I crave for those things which I do not deserve.'

And the messenger's reply was: 'Dionysus has forgiven you, for he knows of your suffering. Go down, therefore, to the River Pactolus and follow it till you reach its source near Mount Timolus. There, where the foaming waters come gushing from the rocks, bathe yourself in the river. The gold will be utterly cleansed from your body and the gift of the Golden Touch will be taken from you. Carry pitchers of these waters and pour them plentifully upon anything you wish to be changed to its erstwhile form.'

Scarcely were the words out of the messenger's mouth when Midas grabbed the largest of the pitchers he could lay his hands on and dashed headlong towards the turbulent waters of the Pactolus. He plunged deep into the rushing river till the gold of his body had turned the sand of the river into sparkling grains. To this very day the sands of that river have retained their golden hue.

Midas felt cleansed not only in body but in heart and mind too. He felt his foolish greed has been washed away together with his Golden Touch. Filling his pitcher, he rushed with all speed to the palace and poured it full over the golden figure of his adored daughter. He hair softened into falling glinting tresses round her little round face, now flushed and rosy. She laughed heartily to see her father pouring water all over her, drenching her pretty dress. And Midas, dripping from head to foot, joined in the merriment, his laughter resonant with gratitude and relief. 'Father dear,' said the child, 'what *are* you doing?' for she had no notion that seconds earlier she had been a lifeless statue.

Midas took her little hand in his and together they splashed water on all the golden roses; how they glowed at the sight of their return to their natural beauty as the exquisite fragrance filled the air around them. Midas sprinkled water over everything his Golden Touch had transformed into the now hated metal until they were all as they had been before.

Soon the king was seated in dry royal robes at the table beside his little daughter, as pretty as a picture in her clean little dress, and they ate the heartiest breakfast ever enjoyed by a king and princess or, for that matter, by any ordinary being on earth.

Jason and the Golden Fleece

I n ancient Greece, many centuries ago, a certain King named Aeson might have been seen wandering among the mountains with his young son, Jason. He had been driven from his throne and kingdom of Iolcos by his cruel, tyrannical brother-in-law, Pelias. After they had trudged many a long mile over marshland and crag, up mountains and down steep valleys, Aeson had to carry his son on his back and he was a very weary man indeed when he at last arrived at a cave at the foot of a mighty cliff where Chiron lived. Now Chiron was a Centaur and like all the Centaurs he was a man down to the waist but below he had the body of a noble horse. And Chiron was wiser and kinder than anyone in the whole world. His white hair fell over his broad shoulders and a long silvery beard half hid his massive chest. Aeson left Jason with Chiron to be looked after and to be brought up in the way a young prince should be brought up and taught all the things a young prince should know. Many kings before had sent their sons to Chiron, for there was nothing he could not teach them. He was the finest player of the harp, he was the deadliest archer, he sang the most haunting songs, he could tell wondrous tales of olden times, and his skill with spear and sword was unsurpassed.

The boy Jason was full of admiration and respect for this amazing teacher and so here, with many other heroes and princes, he grew up to be a strong, handsome young man well versed in the arts of singing, dancing and playing the harp, and skilled in hunting, riding and wrestling, and also in the art of medicine and healing. He was later to become known as Jason the Healer.

But now the time had come for Jason to leave the cave of Chiron and to set out to punish the wicked Pelias for all the wrong he had done to his father Aeson. So, bidding a sad farewell to his wise master, with a spear in each hand and a leopard's skin flung over his shoulder, he set forth on his long travels. On his feet were a pair of richly embroidered sandals, tied with slender golden thongs, which had belonged to his father.

One day as he reached the foot of a lofty mountain he arrived at a veritable raging torrent of a stream, swollen by heavy rains. An old woman, with a peacock on her shoulder, stood on the edge, not daring to cross. Jason, remembering Chiron's words that the strong must help the weak, and although himself hesitant to step into those turbulent waters, offered to carry her across. The old woman was no light weight and Jason had to struggle furiously with the current dashing round his legs and thighs as he stumbled against trunks of trees uprooted by the mighty surge of the waters. His sandalled feet kept sticking to the muddy bed of the stream and just as he was about to reach the opposite bank one sandal left his foot, to be carried relentlessly away. Heaving a sigh of relief, he put the old woman carefully down, but imagine his astonishment when he saw that she had changed into the greatest of all goddesses, Hera, the wife of Zeus. With a promise to help him wherever he went she vanished into thin air, leaving Jason standing there, drenched to the skin, with only one sandal, and breathless with wonder.

Limping wearily on he came at long last to the city of Iolcos. People stopped in the streets to stare at this strange handsome youth with his leopard skin. But when they looked at his feet they began to whisper, 'Look, he wears only one sandal.' The whispers grew to a murmur and very soon you could hear one single cry from all sides, 'The man with one sandal has come. The man with one sandal has come.' When the King heard of his arrival he trembled with fear, for it had been foretold that one day a man wearing only one sandal would come and take away his kingdom. However, he made a great pretence of being pleased to see the stranger and told him he was the very man he had been waiting for. He needed a strong, brave man, daring enough to go to Colchis to bring back the Golden Fleece.

Now Jason knew all about the Golden Fleece. It had come from the back of a wonderful gold-fleeced ram which had saved two children, Phryxus and Helle, from the clutches of their stepmother, who wanted to kill them. The ram had flown away with the two, carrying them on its back. The girl, Helle, had fallen into the sea (which later became known as the Hellespont) but Phryxus had reached Colchis and hung the fleece on the branch of an oak tree, where it lit up the dark woods and shone with a golden light for many miles around. It was now guarded by a terrible sleepless dragon in the royal grove at Colchis. Many heroes had tried in vain to capture the Golden Fleece. To go in quest of it was like marching to certain death. Jason knew all this full well and he knew that the cunning King Pelias hoped to get rid of him by suggesting that he should go and capture it. At that very instant he could hear the voice of the great goddess Hera (that same goddess, who, disguised as an old woman, had tested his courage and kindness by asking him to carry her across the turbulent stream) whisper to him, 'Be not afraid, Jason, I shall help you.' So he looked King Pelias straight in the eye and said calmly, 'I will go and capture the Golden Fleece and will bring it back here to this palace – or perish in the attempt – but on one condition.'

'And what is that condition, Jason?' asked the King.

'That you return to my father his rightful kingdom,' was Jason's reply.

'I will. I swear most solemnly that I will,' said the King loudly, but inwardly he thought, Well, that is the end of him, and he smiled to himself at the clever way he thought he had trapped the brave youth into undertaking this dread mission.

The first thing Jason did when he rose next morning at the break of dawn was to ask the advice of the enchanted tree known as the Talking Oak which stood towering, over a hundred feet high, in the centre of an ancient wood in Dodona.

'What must I do', he asked, 'to gain the Golden Fleece?' Through the myriads of rustling leaves Jason heard the clear reply:

'Go to Argus the Shipbuilder and ask him to build you a galley with fifty oars.' In the city of Iolcos Jason did indeed find this famed shipwright, who immediately set to work, helped by innumerable apprentices. When the ship, the *Argo*, was completed, people came from far and wide to admire it, for no ship so large and heavy had ever been built before. Then Jason went once more to ask the advice of the Talking Oak. This time it told him to hack off one of its boughs and to have it carved into a figurehead for the *Argo*. When it was finished Jason was surprised to hear a voice coming from the mouth of the figurehead.

'Send out heralds', said the voice, 'to all the heroes and princes who were your schoolmates and playfellows in Chiron's cave and get forty-nine of them to accompany you in your quest for the Golden Fleece.'

So messengers were dispatched throughout all the cities and towns of Greece.

'Who will dare,' cried the messengers, 'who will dare help Jason row his vessel and be bold enough to face dangers too terrible to describe and bring back the Golden Fleece to Iolcos?'

Every youth with spirit was eager to take on this impossible quest, but Jason could select only forty-nine who had already proved themselves in dangerous combat. Among them were the mighty Hercules, Theseus, and the twins Castor and Pollux, and Orpheus, who played on his lyre and sang with such haunting charm that the wildest of beasts would sit down tamely before him and stare dreamily into the distance. And there were times when he played more stirring tunes and then whole forests of trees would uproot themselves and great rocks and boulders would come careering madly down the hills.

Now they were ready to launch the *Argo* down the beach, but she proved too heavy for even them to move and her keel sank into the sand. So once more Jason had to ask the advice of the magic figurehead – the bough of the Talking Oak.

'Let Orpheus play gently upon the lyre,' said the figurehead. So the heroes waited and held the pine-trunk rollers firmly while Orpheus played and sang. And lo! gradually there was a stirring in all the ship's timbers, and then a mighty heaving from stem to stern and finally the *Argo* sprang on to the rollers and leapt forward into the surging sea. And so the good ship *Argo* was launched.

Then, having provided her well with food and water, they all took their places at the oars and rowed away to the shouting and cheering of the people watching from the cliff tops.

The first stop on their voyage was at the cave of Chiron, their old master, who gave them his blessing and good advice. Soon they were to meet their first peril, the dreaded rocks of the Black Sea, which actually moved and crashed into one another, ready to crush all comers. They waited in vain for an opening in the rocks and it seemed that they would never get through. Then suddenly a heron came flying mast-high towards the rocks and hovered and soared around for a while as though waiting for a passage through. Jason realized that the bird had been sent to them by Hera to act as a pilot. They saw the heron fly swiftly through in safety just as the mighty rocks came crashing together and caught a feather from its tail. Then the rocks parted as if riven asunder by the shock of the collision and now our heroes bent over their oars with all their might and rowed safely through before the rocks could come together again.

And now they rowed further and further eastward along the southern shores of the Euxine Sea and after many more breathtaking perils and adventures and many a narrow escape from death, the Argonauts espied in the distance the gleaming gold of the palace of King Aietes in the city of Colchis where, hidden among the woods, was the Golden Fleece.

The King was told of their approach and he came down to the riverside in his golden chariot, followed by a train of servants and fierce-looking soldiers. He was a splendid sight, this Child of the Sun, in robes of heavy gold tissue and with the jewels of his crown flashing fire. He did indeed look like his father, the sun himself.

But Jason and his heroes were not afraid.

'We have not come to plunder your land,' Jason said calmly to the King, 'but to take back the Golden Fleece to Iolcos. If you wish to fight us, then fight we must, but I must warn you that my comrades are heroes of great renown and that some are sons of the Immortals.'

Much to Jason's surprise, Aietes's reply was mild. 'Why should we fight?' he asked. 'Far better to choose one of your best men and let him carry out the duties I will require of him. If he is successful, I shall give him the opportunity to win the Golden Fleece.'

Jason, as leader of the Argonauts, accepted the challenge for himself, but little did he imagine what he would have to achieve to gain his objective.

First, he must tame two fire-eating bulls and plough a four-acre field with them.

Second, he must sow that field with a dragon's teeth, which would immediately spring up into fully armed men.

[69]

Third, he must fight and conquer these armed warriors.

Now, Aietes's beautiful daughter, Medea, who was also an enchantress, had fallen in love with Jason as soon as she had set eyes on him. She did not want him to die. So that evening she sent a messenger-boy to the shore where Jason, with his men, was keeping watch over their good ship the *Argo*

'Go quickly to the Palace,' whispered the lad to Jason, 'where the Princess Medea wishes to speak with you urgently.'

When Jason saw the Princess he felt he was in the presence of someone who was both very beautiful and very terrible.

'Jason,' she said, 'if you trust me and if you are indeed fearless, I can tell you how to tame the fiery bulls, sow the dragon's teeth and win the Golden Fleece. For I am an enchantress and I know all about the old woman you carried across the stream, the Talking Oak and the adventures you have had in coming to Colchis.' Jason listened eagerly, quite overwhelmed by the Princess's beauty.

'Here is a charmed ointment,' continued Medea, handing him a golden box. 'If you smear this over your body the bulls' fiery breath cannot harm you.' She then handed him a basket containing the dragon's teeth and led him to the field where the bulls were quietly grazing. As Medea left him, Jason tiptoed nearer and nearer to the bulls, and he could clearly see four streams of fiery vapour oozing out from their nostrils. He halted and smeared his body with the enchanted ointment and went boldly on. Hearing his footsteps the bulls sprang up with a fierce roar and came charging towards him, their breath scorching the pasture before them. But the heat did not touch Jason and his heart was brave. Just as they were about to toss him high up into the air, he grabbed one of them by the horn and the other by the tail and held them in a grip of iron. And suddenly they were just ordinary bulls, breathing in the ordinary way. Jason's courage and Medea's ointment had broken the spell. Jason then yoked the bulls, harnessed them to the plough lying in a corner of the field and ploughed the whole field in the expert way that his master Chiron had taught him. He then scattered the dragon's teeth far and wide over the ploughed black earth and immediately there began to sprout up, helmets first, dark, fierce-looking warriors, one for each tooth. They formed ranks and charged as one man towards Jason, brandishing their flaming swords.

'Pick up a stone and throw it among them,' called Medea's voice from the distance. This Jason did and the stone bounded off the helmet of one warrior and crashed into another's. Then there was complete confusion among them and instead of attacking Jason they all began fighting one another. And that was how Jason left them.

Early next morning he went to the Palace of Aietes and told the King that he had tamed the fiery bulls, ploughed the field, sown the dragon's teeth and left the armed warriors killing one another. This put the King in a state of extreme terror, for he realized at once that his beautiful enchantress daughter had helped Jason to achieve all this and that now Jason would be perfectly capable of slaying the Dragon which guarded the Golden Fleece.

'You have not acted fairly,' he said sternly to Jason. 'And so I cannot allow you to try to win the Fleece.'

As Jason was leaving the Palace, wondering what to do next, he was stopped by Medea. 'Jason,' she said, 'my father has decreed that I must die. He also plans to burn your fine galley and to slay all your comrades. But if you trust me I shall help you. Wait for me here at midnight.'

Jason replied: 'You shall not die. We will win the Golden Fleece and you will return with me to be my Queen in Iolcos by the sea.'

At the appointed hour the pair made their way stealthily towards the Sacred Grove. Suddenly Jason stopped with a gasp of amazement. He had caught his first glimpse of the dazzling radiance of the Golden Fleece. So eager was he to see its full splendour that he would have rushed forward had not Medea held his arm. 'Beware!' she warned, 'have you forgotten the dragon?' It was at that moment that the scaly black head of the dreaded monster came into view, its forked tongue darting and hissing as it heard their footsteps. Medea drew out a gold box from the folds of her dress and flung its contents straight into the dragon's steaming jaws. With a furious flick of its enormous tail the beast surged forward and – fell motionless. Jason leapt lightly forward over the dragon's body and pulled the Golden Fleece from the tree. Then he and Medea rushed back to the shore where the *Argo* was beached, and they all made merry with food and wine to celebrate their great capture. But their rejoicings were soon cut short by the voice of the figurehead on the *Argo*.

'Make haste, Jason,' it said, 'make haste, flee for your lives.' Jason looked up and saw the glittering chariot of Aietes, followed by innumerable warriors, speeding down towards the shore. As one

man all fifty heroes leapt to their oars as Jason held aloft the wondrous Golden Fleece. Aietes and his men hurled poisoned arrows in impotent rage at the scudding galleon. But the Argonauts warded them off with their shields and Orpheus took up his lyre and sang a song of praise to the heroes. And to this sweet music the good ship *Argo* sped westwards towards Iolcos to claim the kingdom for Jason and his queen.

Mr Wind, Miss Rain, and the
Tiny Golden Kitchen

Long ago in Brittany there lived a poor miller named Jean-Pierre.
All he owned was his mill, a ramshackle little hut and a vegetable garden where he grew cabbages and carrots. Fortune did not
smile upon him. He could see other windmills on the hillsides whir-
ling round and round but his own mill was still because the wind kept
away from it. Down in the valley it rained in plenty while the vegetables in his own garden withered from drought. All Jean-Pierre
could do was to go on repeating, 'Alas, Mr Wind, won't you come
and blow my windmill? And you, Miss Rain, won't you pour down
into my garden so that I too can earn a bit of a living?'

But his complaints weren't much use. Mr Wind didn't listen and
Miss Rain didn't seem to bother much either. To cheer him up in his
misery the miller married a pretty girl named Claudine who was as
poor as he was but who was a good housewife and not afraid of hard
work. She cleaned out the thatch, repaired the linen, tidied the
house, reared chickens and took the eggs to market. Before long they
had a baby son whom they named Pierrot and things began to look a
little brighter. But what Claudine had saved up since her marriage
was hardly enough to buy a cradle or baby clothes. She was down to
her last farthing. On top of all this she fell ill and they had to call the

village doctor. Jean-Pierre neglected his work so that he could look after Claudine. In short, Jean-Pierre and his wife suddenly found themselves as poor as church mice.

One night as he sat watching his wife asleep in bed, Jean-Pierre began to think about his wretched situation. If it was just me, he thought, I wouldn't complain. I'm sturdy enough to stand cold and hunger. But my wife needs warmth, good food and medicine and I haven't even enough wood to make a fire, nor meat to make a broth nor money to pay the chemist. I love my Claudine and my child more dearly than all the treasures on earth. If only the Wind would deign to blow upon my mill . . . if only . . . if only . . . I could find a way out of my woes.

As he spoke these words Jean-Pierre saw the flame of the candle flicker and heard the rusty weather-cock turning above the thatched roof of his dwelling. The wind was beginning to blow. Jean-Pierre sped up to his mill, fed enough grain to the millstone to last the whole night, loosened the brakes which kept the sails still and all at once the windmill started to turn and to grind the grain and to change it to bran and flour. Then he went straight back to his sleeping wife and rubbed his hands in glee in anticipation of the happy news he would tell her when she woke.

Meantime the candle nearly went out and he had to put it behind a curtain because there were so many chinks and crevices in the cottage that strong draughts of air kept creeping in from all sides. The windows shook, the door stirred uneasily on its hinges and cinders from the fireplace flew across the room. At the height of this stormy din Jean-Pierre thought he could hear the spirits of the Wind whispering in his ear: 'Let us whistle,' they seemed to say, 'let us whistle through this broken tile. Let us whine and moan through this hole. Let us wheeze down the chimney.'

The miller, though astonished by these mysterious voices, was not in the least bit frightened and he gave them this reply: 'Whistle, moan, and wheeze as much as you please as long as you keep my windmill turning.'

At that very moment the door-latch sprang up, the door opened wide and an extraordinary figure appeared. He looked more like a genie than a real person. His body could bend in any direction; it was supple and elastic. His eyes had a phosphorescent gleam. His enormous chest made a noise like a blacksmith's bellows. The two wings on his shoulders were too large to spread out in the room. A red cloak of gossamer flimsiness floated about him, making so many folds that it was difficult to discern the exact outlines of his body. His feet skimmed the ground and moved without having to walk.

'Give me a chair,' he said to Jean-Pierre. 'I must rest awhile before I resume my journey.'

The miller brought forward his best straw chair. 'Sit down, sir,' he said, 'and rest here as long as you wish.'

'Fear nothing,' said the stranger, 'I am Mr Wind, to whom you have prayed several times. You will not be surprised to see me rather breathless when I tell you that in less than one month I have visited the entire length of the Brittany coast and blown over vast tracts of the Atlantic Ocean. Your own lord and master, the Seigneur to whom you pay your rent and whose castle is not far from here, was unwilling to let me in. His servants have secured the doors with powerful bolts and its windows with solid shutters. I barely managed to penetrate an odd stairway by way of a skylight in a turret. But I had my own back on the warders who mount guard in the long corridors of the castle; I kept overturning their sentry-boxes. But when I arrived at your house I found a door with holes that let in the daylight, windows cracked and the door latch loose. All I had to do was give a gentle push to your door and I was inside your cottage. That's the way I like houses to be! You only have one shabby straw chair but how courteously you offered it to me. I am grateful to you for your welcoming hospitality. Ask me any favour, Jean-Pierre, and I shall gladly grant it.'

'All I ask, Mr Wind,' said the miller, 'is that you blow on my windmill a few hours each day.'

'My poor Jean-Pierre,' replied Mr Wind, 'I'm not allowed out every day. Miss Rain has possession of the sky for a third of the year and ungratefully drives me out as soon as I've swept away the clouds. As for the sun, his relations with me are even worse. I have to live locked up in my cave for months on end. But what I can and will do is to send you light breezes and minor spirits who, on my orders, go out and inspect the countryside, and I shall command them not to forget your windmill. Whenever you are in difficulties come and see me in my cave and I shall come to your aid. I live up there, right at the summit of the Southern Mountain. But now I have to leave immediately for Paris where I'm due to knock down some dozen chimneys.

And in about half an hour I must be back in my home because here comes Miss Rain right on my heels. Farewell, Jean-Pierre.'

And with those words he rushed to the door in one gust, opened out his great wings and disappeared. Very soon the whistlings and wheezings became quieter and quieter and finally were silent. The miller realized that the wind had completed his journey but the minor spirits which he had left behind were sufficiently strong to keep his windmill turning.

Shortly after Mr Wind had left it began to rain, gently at first but soon in torrents. Jean-Pierre was sure he could hear the voices of the spirits of Rain. 'Let us fall,' they seemed to say, 'let us fall on this thatched roof. Let us moisten the whole of this house. Let us water those cabbage leaves. Let us, little raindrops that we are, fall and make everything wet.'

Jean-Pierre was not frightened by these voices. He answered them: 'Fall, moisten, water everything you can and tomorrow my garden will be greener and my vegetables will thrive.'

Now Mr Wind had left without closing the door properly. Through this slight opening Jean-Pierre saw a very tall and unusual-looking lady making a grand entry. She looked more like a fairy than a lady, though. Her body was somehow hazy and vague, and her face somewhat worn as though she was recovering from an illness. Her hair, completely straight, without the slightest wave or curl, hung right down to her heels. Her eyes were veiled by two streams of tears running down her cheeks and her nose seemed slightly swollen as though she was suffering from a cold in the head. Her glistening silken scarf was adorned with the seven colours of the rainbow. The lady advanced majestically into the room hardly moving her feet. Extending her arms she gave a huge yawn and seemed overcome, but by boredom rather than weariness.

'Give me a chair,' she said to Jean-Pierre. 'I must rest awhile before I go down into the valley.'

'Pray sit down, Madam,' said the miller offering a chair. 'Fear nothing,' replied the lady. 'I am Miss Rain, to whom you have often addressed your requests. Five minutes ago I was more than half a mile above the earth and that is why I'm feeling a little dazed after my descent. The Lord of the Manor, the grand Seigneur your neighbour, shut his doors and windows in my face but I had my own back! I simply drenched his warders to the skin. But with your house it's

[77]

different. I found crevices in the walls, broken windows and the door open. I like your cottage and I shall not forget your warm welcome. If I can be of any service, do not hesitate to call upon me. Ask of me whatever you like.'

'Miss Rain,' began the miller, 'what could I ask of you except that you be kind enough to pour rain upon the vegetables in my kitchen garden two or three times a week.'

'Alas, my friend,' said the lady, 'it is not in my power to gallivant across the world as I please. The good old days of the flood are past. Mr Sun is more powerful than I and sees to it that I am confined to my grotto whenever he can. As for Madam Moon, ever since the beginning of the world I have tried to discover whether she is on my side or not and I have not yet been able to find out. But with the help of some astronomer friends, I hope, in the next three or four thousand years, to establish precisely what her intentions are. For two-thirds of the year I am locked up but I shall send you my early morning dews as well as small cloudlets, to whom I sometimes entrust the keys to the fields between the sunny intervals. But now I must set out for the plains of Normandy, which are in dire need of water. The sun will have soon dried up all my valiant efforts. Farewell, Jean-Pierre. My dwelling is in the grotto on the Western Sea Shore.'

Jean-Pierre then came out of his house and went to the mill. There was enough to fill two sacks with flour. Then he ran into the garden and he picked lettuces and cabbages which had grown there. He took the flour to the farmer who paid him well and sold the vegetables in the market. His wife was still asleep when he got back home, a bundle of wood on his shoulder, money in his pocket and a stock of groceries in his basket.

Jean-Pierre's wife hadn't heard either the wind or the rain. She was most surprised to learn that the mill had been turning during the night and to see the money and groceries her husband had brought home. She was already feeling much better at hearing the good news. However, Jean-Pierre had not told her a word about his two extraordinary visitors. Claudine, he thought to himself, is much cleverer than I am but she is also a bit talkative. She might give my secret away to all the gossiping neighbours.

And now, day after day, the mill went on working and the vegetable garden felt the benefit of the dew. Jean-Pierre kept the house nice and warm and fed his family well. Claudine regained her old vigour and young Pierrot grew strong and rosy-cheeked.

One day the Lord of the Manor happened to pass by. Now this Seigneur was a particularly hard-hearted man. His chief pleasure was hoarding money and in order to get as much as he could he burdened his peasants with heavy taxes. When the miller saw him he was frightened, for such visits never resulted in any good.

'Hey there, Jean-Pierre!' shouted the Seigneur without bothering to alight from his horse, 'you owe me six months' taxes. My steward will call on you tomorrow morning to collect those ten sovereigns.'

'My lord,' replied the miller, 'please allow me another three months. My wife has been sick and if I pay you now I won't have a penny left for her or my son.'

'I will not even grant you three days,' said the flint-hearted man. 'If you do not pay me tomorrow I shall evict you from your cottage and you will be put to work in my fields where, if you are lazy, you will be beaten.'

The Seigneur galloped off without listening any further to Jean-Pierre's pleadings. The next morning his steward arrived and Jean-Pierre was obliged to give ten sovereigns – which was all he had managed to save. And so all the efforts of Mr Wind and Miss Rain were wasted.

Claudine began to weep bitterly and Jean-Pierre tried his best to console her.

'Don't cry, dear,' he said, 'not everyone is as wicked as the Seigneur. Just get me my hobnailed boots, my stick and woollen coat; I have to make a call and don't worry if I don't get back till late. I shall have some good news to report.'

Claudine could guess that her husband was hiding some secret from her. She wiped away her tears and pestered her husband with questions but all in vain. He set out on his journey and after a long, long trudge through the fields and meadows Jean-Pierre arrived at long last at the foot of the Southern Mountain. For three hours he climbed through dense pine woods until he found himself facing a vast stretch of deserted heathland at the foot of steep rocks, and were it not for his hobnailed boots and stout stick he would never have reached the top. He reached the summit of the mountain just before sunset. He then saw an entrance to the cave which he took to be the dwelling of Mr Wind and he felt very nervous when he found how deep and dark it turned out to be. But he plucked up courage and groped his way along with his stick. But he had hardly taken more than twenty steps when he heard the voices of the little spirits.

'Let us blow upon this stranger,' said the voices. 'Let us take away his coat and hat.' But Jean-Pierre held fast to his hat with one hand and with the other his woollen coat. Finally he glimpsed light and recognized Mr Wind sitting at a table eating his dinner. Two will-o'-the-wisps flitted around him to give him light, while other spirits brought him dishes of food and flagons of wine.

'Who goes there?' asked Mr Wind.

'It is I,' replied the miller. 'I, Jean-Pierre. Your Excellency was gracious enough to take a rest in my house a month ago.'

'Well, what is it you wish?'

'I don't know, sir,' stammered the miller, 'but my awe of you makes me falter in my speech. From the time that you deigned to favour my mill, I was able to save ten sovereigns. But now this morning the Lord of the Manor sent his steward and robbed me of them, pretending I owed him taxes. I implore your Excellency to come to my aid.'

'I have no time to concern myself with your affairs,' replied the moody Mr Wind. 'Make an effort to tell me what it is you wish and say it in as few words as possible.'

'Give me whatever it pleases you to give me as long as it prevents me and my family dying of hunger.'

'You shall not die of hunger,' said Mr Wind in a rather gentler tone. Then he gave an order: 'Let this creature be given a small cask of silver.'

A spirit with bat's wings at once brought out a pretty silver cask. A second spirit brought a wand, also of silver, which it placed on the table.

'Take this cask and wand,' said Mr Wind. 'When you reach home strike the cask with the wand and you will see what happens. And now kindly be off and leave me to dine in peace!'

Night had fallen when Jean-Pierre left Mr Wind's cave. He nearly broke his neck stumbling among the rocks. He tore his woollen coat in the bushes and got his feet soaked in a marsh in spite of his hobnail boots. But never did he let go of his cask and wand. When, at last, the miller reached his dwelling, his wife was in a state of great anxiety.

'What is this?' asked Claudine when she saw the little cask. 'I knew you were hiding some important secret from me. You must tell me all about this mystery right away. Are there any precious stones in this cask? Even if there is nothing inside it, the silver alone must be worth at least one thousand sovereigns.'

The miller then told her all about the visit he had received from Mr Wind and how he had promised him his protection and given him the cask and wand. He begged her not to breathe a word of it to her neighbours.

'Perhaps', interrupted Claudine, 'you can see how wrong you were not to let me in on the secret from the beginning. I could have given you sound advice. Instead of standing there gaping in front of Mr Wind when he asked you what you wanted, I would have told you to ask for ten thousand sovereigns. And you would have come back with all that lovely money instead of this silver cask which we now have to dispose of.'

'Who knows?' replied the miller. 'My cask may perhaps be worth even more than you think. Let us put it to the test.'

Jean-Pierre placed the cask upright on the table and with a trembling hand touched the top of it with the silver wand. Immediately the cask opened out in two parts like the door of a cupboard. On one side there was a little kitchen and on the other a miniature pantry. In the kitchen there were roasting spits no thicker than needles, cauldrons as big as thimbles, and ridiculously tiny saucepans and frying pans. A cook no taller than three inches in height, his chef's bonnet cocked over one ear, and two small kitchen boys, were bustling about in front of ovens. They were fanning the fire with bellows and keeping an eye on the spit while the chef was sampling the sauces. Other servants were roasting turkeys the size of bees and hens as tiny as flies; others were drying fish slimmer than newborn silk-worms and cutting cabbage hearts which looked like pin heads. Meanwhile two other diminutive servants were putting away the crockery. They wiped the tiny china plates and glasses and were filling bottles with two drops of wine and the crystal carafes with two droplets of water. Before you could say Jack Robinson the dinner was ready.

The miller and his wife stood in blank amazement as they watched this busy little world and their astonishment knew no bounds when they saw the two midget servants leave the cask, hop on to the table and set down the steaming dishes, lay the table for two and place the bottles and carafes in the proper place. Then they placed the first course at one end of the table and the second in the opposite corner, not forgetting the dessert, after which they returned to their pantry. The silver cask then closed promptly and there was nothing further to view. However, at the same instant the dishes on the table became proper-sized dishes, the roast chickens became full-sized, the tiny fish substantial portions, the miniature bottles normal bottles filled with fine wines and all the cutlery and napery just as they should be for normal-sized people. Jean-Pierre and his wife found themselves facing a magnificent repast for two, but sufficient for at least four. They sat down and ate their fill for they were very hungry. The stews and soups were perfect and the meat done to a turn.

Three times did Jean-Pierre drink to the health of Mr Wind and as the wine was on the strong side the miller lay down feeling a little dizzy, fell asleep at once and snored like a humming-top. Claudine went to bed too but she could only toss and turn in the bed without falling asleep, so eager was she to get up to tell her neighbour, the milkmaid, all about their exciting adventure. And when she actually did this the next morning, the milkmaid's eyes nearly popped right out with astonishment. As soon as the miller's wife had left, the milkmaid placed her basket on her head and went to deliver cream and butter to the Manor. And she didn't forget to tell the whole story to the cook there. And the cook told the story to the valet, and the valet, as he helped his master to get dressed, told him what had happened to the miller. The Lord of the Manor lost no time in scheming how to get hold of the silver cask; he immediately mounted his horse and rode off to the mill. When he got there Jean-Pierre had just woken up.

'Jean-Pierre,' began the Seigneur 'Mr Wind, who is one of my friends, has just informed me that he has given you a small silver cask, which contains a magic kitchen. Why on earth would you want roast turkey in your broken-down old hut with its worm-eaten bits of furniture? It would be far better to have your tumbledown cottage repaired by a good carpenter and to buy yourself some respectable clothing, and a few comfortable armchairs. I offer you ten thousand sovereigns for that silver cask.'

'My lord,' replied Jean-Pierre, 'when I've spent my ten thousand sovereigns I won't have anything left, while if I keep my little cask I and my family will have enough to eat for the rest of our lives.'

[82]

'Nonsense!' snapped the greedy Seigneur. 'Don't you think it's important to own your own house and cultivate your own fields?'

'That is true,' replied Jean-Pierre. 'My wife told me off for not asking Mr Wind for ten thousand sovereigns. And since you are offering me that sum I am willing to accept.'

'Well said!' replied the cunning schemer. 'Your wife is a clever woman. Here are one hundred sovereigns which is all I have on my person at the moment. My steward will bring the rest in a fortnight. Now give me your silver barrel.'

The miller surrendered his cask and accepted the hundred sovereigns.

Jean-Pierre couldn't wait for his wife to get back home to tell her of his great deal with the Lord of the Manor. But instead of welcoming it she began to moan and tear her hair in rage.

'Ah, Holy Mother!' she exclaimed, 'Why did I have to marry a man who can be so easily duped! Wretch that I am to be burdened with a husband who is such a hopeless dolt!'

Jean-Pierre grew fearfully angry. 'Fickle woman!' he cried. 'Didn't you rebuke me yourself for not asking Mr Wind for ten thousand sovereigns *instead* of the silver cask?'

'You foolish ninny,' replied his wife. 'When I said that, I didn't know what was inside that marvellous toy. Can't you even see that those little creatures have left us all this splendid crockery and brilliant cutlery and napery? They did not put them back into the cask. Every day they would have left us these lovely silver spoons and knives and forks, and we could have sold them to the goldsmith. Why does one want fields and cattle in the first place? Is it not in order to be able to afford roast chicken? And since we had roast chicken what was the point of owning fields and cattle. Fields can be ruined by storms, and cattle can die of disease. But with our little silver cask we could be certain of never being short of anything. The Lord of the Manor has made a fool of you. He tricked you into believing that he knew Mr Wind. And he probably won't pay the rest of the ten thousand sovereigns that he promised you.'

Jean-Pierre was beginning to realize how foolish he had been but he wasn't prepared to admit it. He got even more angry. 'It's all your fault,' he shouted at his wife. 'It was through your gossiping tongue that our secret was discovered.'

Instead of admitting her fault, Claudine redoubled her scoldings.

[83]

She called her husband a blockhead and he called her a nitwit and they went on arguing and quarrelling for hours. But in the end they managed to make peace because deep down the miller was a good husband and Claudine a worthy wife.

What Claudine had forseen happened. Once he had the little cask in his hands the Lord of the Manor did not worry one wit about his promise to Jean-Pierre. When the miller turned up at the castle gates with a promissory note in his hands he was roughly dismissed and was told it was an unforgivable insolence on his part to dare ask money from the Master himself. All Jean-Pierre had, therefore, were the hundred sovereigns instead of the ten thousand he had been promised. And his fury and frustration were all the greater when he learned that the magic cask was made use of daily in the Manor House, and that it served up the most magnificent dinners for as many guests as the master felt like asking. The Lord of the Manor had no further need of a cook and so he and the kitchen boys were sacked. Each day the midget servants supplied new napery, cutlery and crockery and soon there was such an accumulation of them in the grand house that they didn't know where to put them or what to do with them. Jean-Pierre swore by the almighty heavens that he would never again allow himself to be duped like that or to be tempted by treacherous offers from the cruel Seigneur. And Claudine promised never again to gossip away her secrets to her neighbours.

With the hundred sovereigns the miller had a few repairs done to his cottage and bought some household utensils, and by saving very carefully managed to eke out a living for the rest of the year. By that time he and his wife were in very low spirits. The very thought of the good life that they had so rapidly lost poisoned their lives and they were left more wretched than ever before.

Finally, Jean-Pierre decided that the time had come to pay a visit to Miss Rain.

Without saying a word to his wife, he put on his hobnailed boots and his woollen coat and set out, stick in hand, on his long journey. And what a dreary journey it was! But at last he reached the Western Sea Shore and the grotto, which was enshrouded in deep mist. Little spirits flitted round about with their fin-like wings. As he passed they sprayed him with water and whispered, 'Let us drench this bold creature. Let us seep through his woollen coat and pierce his boots with fine jets of water.' But Jean-Pierre simply pulled his coat collar more firmly and snuggly round his neck and walked bravely on till he reached the end of the grotto. There he found Miss Rain surrounded by grey nymphs. Miss Rain was stocking up her larder. Her little spirits, one by one, were bringing in the minute drops of water which the sun had evaporated from the sea, the rivers, the woodlands and marshlands. The nymphs caught the drops in small golden goblets and threw them into a large reservoir. When Miss Rain saw Jean-Pierre she started to yawn, blew her nose and said dolefully, 'Who is this tiresome person disturbing me when I'm busy?'

'Madam,' replied the miller, 'I'm Jean-Pierre in whose house you were gracious enough to take a little rest some time ago. You then promised to help me in my hour of need.' He then poured out his heart and told her the whole sad story: about the little kitchen and how he had been tricked by the scheming Lord of the Manor.

Miss Rain listened in a sort of drowsy silence. 'I have just the thing for you,' she said suddenly, as though waking up from a dream. At a wave of her sylph-like arm two little spirits tiptoed in, carrying a cask of gleaming gold and the minutest golden wand.

'Take this, Jean-Pierre,' she said, 'and you will see what you will see. But . . .' and here Miss Rain paused, 'you must also carry with you, IN YOUR MIND, these enchanted words:

> *Right is Right*
> *And Wrong is Wrong,*
> *These wise words complete my song.*

Jean-Pierre bowed and made off as quickly as he could with the cask and wand – lest Miss Rain should change her mind.

Now the clever Claudine had guessed that her husband had gone on a secret mission and she waited impatiently for his return. When she beheld the gleaming golden cask she clapped her hands and danced with joy.

'Now we'll be rich for the rest of our lives,' she exclaimed. 'We'll have golden forks and spoons now, not silver ones. We shall sell them and with the money we'll buy great estates, castles and houses. And even if the Seigneur were to offer us hundreds of thousands of sovereigns, we wouldn't part with it. Hurry! Hurry! Hurry! Jean-Pierre! and touch the cask with the wand for I haven't prepared any dinner. I *knew* you'd come back with something very special.'

Jean-Pierre placed the cask on the ground and gave it a quiet tap

with the wand. A door opened . . . To their horror a dense black smoke gushed out filling the room up to the ceiling But worse was to come. The smoke then took on a human shape, with an enormous head larger than a pumpkin, a most hideous face and a body thicker than the trunk of an oak. It grew and grew into a terrifying giant, puffing the suffocating smoke into Jean-Pierre's face and went on chasing him round the room till Claudine could barely recognize him.

'Didn't Miss Rain warn you about this?' she screamed.

'No!' panted Jean-Pierre. 'She only told me to remember the words.

> *Right is Right*
> *And Wrong is Wrong,*
> *These wise words complete my song.*

These words were scarcely out of Jean-Pierre's mouth than the smoking giant recoiled into the cask and the horrid smoke dispersed completely.

Now the two of them clearly understood *just what had to be done.* Claudine lost no time making sure that word got round that they now had a *golden* cask, more beautiful than the silver one. In no time at all the Lord of the Manor was at the miller's door, begging him, imploring him, to sell this golden cask. His offer of money was doubled in a twinkling, then just as soon trebled. So now he promised seventy thousand sovereigns. But Jean-Pierre declared firmly:

'The cask stays with me, my lord, till the money is right here, in *my* pocket.'

The Seigneur straight away sent for all the money and triumphantly left, clasping the golden cask and the tiny wand securely in his hands. He wanted to gaze at its treasures in the secrecy of his own private chamber and he made his way there with all speed.

He placed the cask with great care on a small table and gave one tap . . . two taps . . . with the little wand and . . . out sprang the giant, bellowing thick, grimy black smoke straight into the face of the Lord of the Manor. He rushed from the room, darted down the back staircase but to no avail. The giant pursued him relentlessly, all the time puffing out the filthy smoke which completely surrounded the hapless victim, almost completely blinding him.

Where on earth could he escape to hide his shame? Who could he turn to for help? In utter despair he ran to the miller's cottage. But

Jean-Pierre, more wary this time, was determined to teach the Lord of the Manor a lesson, and made sure he spoke only the first part of the magic verse,

> *Right is Right*
> *And Wrong is Wrong,*

without completing it. The consequence was that the smoking giant continued to pursue the Seigneur all around the house, while Jean-Pierre and Claudine kept on repeating the first two lines. At last the Lord of the Manor realized that this chase would go on for ever and ever . . . until the enchanted little kitchen was returned to its rightful owner. And in no time at all the silver cask together with the diminutive little kitchen inside it – miniature pantry, spits no bigger than needles, cauldrons the size of thimbles, ridiculously tiny saucepans and frying-pans, the minute chef and kitchen boys, turkeys no larger than bees and all the rest of the mouth-watering goodies – were all back where they belonged. And in the possession of the good miller and his wife every single thing, except of course the food and the kitchen boys, turned to gold. Then, and only then, did Jean-Pierre and Claudine break into joyous song:

> *Right is Right*
> *And Wrong is Wrong,*
> *These wise words complete my song.*

The Happy Prince

High above the city, on a tall column, stood the statue of the Happy Prince. He was gilded all over with thin leaves of fine gold, for eyes he had two bright sapphires, and a large red ruby glowed on his sword-hilt.

He was very much admired indeed. 'He is as beautiful as a weathercock,' remarked one of the Town Councillors who wished to gain a reputation for having artistic tastes; 'only not quite so useful,' he added, fearing lest people should think him unpractical, which he really was not.

'Why can't you be like the Happy Prince?' asked a sensible mother of her little boy who was crying for the moon. 'The Happy Prince never dreams of crying for anything.'

'I am glad there is someone in the world who is quite happy,' muttered a disappointed man as he gazed at the wonderful statue.

'He looks just like an angel,' said the Charity Children as they came out of the cathedral in their bright scarlet cloaks and their clean white pinafores.

'How do you know?' said the Mathematical Master. 'You have never seen one.'

'Ah! but we have, in our dreams,' answered the children: and the

Mathematical Master frowned and looked very severe, for he did not approve of children dreaming.

One night there flew over the city a little Swallow. His friends had gone away to Egypt six weeks before, but he had stayed behind, for he was in love with the most beautiful Reed. He had met her early in the spring as he was flying down the river after a big yellow moth, and had been so attracted by her slender waist that he had stopped to talk to her.

'Shall I love you?' said the Swallow, who liked to come to the point at once, and the Reed made him a low bow. So he flew round and round her, touching the water with his wings, and making silver ripples. This was his courtship, and it lasted all through the summer.

'It is a ridiculous attachment,' twittered the other Swallows. 'She has no money, and far too many relations'; and indeed the river was quite full of Reeds. Then, when the autumn came, they all flew away.

After they had gone he felt lonely, and began to tire of his lady-love. 'She has no conversation,' he said, 'and I am afraid that she is a coquette, for she is always flirting with the wind.' And certainly, whenever the wind blew, the Reed made the most graceful curtseys. 'I admit that she is domestic,' he continued, 'but I love travelling, and my wife, consequently, should love travelling also.'

'Will you come away with me?' he said finally to her, but the Reed shook her head, she was so attached to her home.

'You have been trifling with me,' he cried, 'I am off to the Pyramids. Goodbye!' and he flew away.

All day long he flew, and at night-time he arrived at the city. 'Where shall I put up?' he said. 'I hope the town has made preparations.'

Then he saw the statue on the tall column.

'I will put up there,' he cried: 'it is a fine position with plenty of fresh air.' So he alighted just between the feet of the Happy Prince.

'I have a golden bedroom,' he said softly to himself as he looked round, and he prepared to go to sleep; but just as he was putting his head under his wing a large drop of water fell on him.

'What a curious thing!' he cried: 'there is not a single cloud in the sky, the stars are quite clear and bright, and yet it is raining. The climate in the north of Europe is really dreadful. The Reed used to like the rain, but that was merely her selfishness.'

Then another drop fell.

'What is the use of a statue if it cannot keep the rain off?' he said. 'I must look for a good chimney-pot,' and he determined to fly away.

But before he had opened his wings, a third drop fell, and he looked up and saw – Ah! what did he see?

The eyes of the Happy Prince were filled with tears, and tears were running down his golden cheeks. His face was so beautiful in the moonlight that the little Swallow was filled with pity.

'Who are you?' he said.

'I am the Happy Prince.'

'Why are you weeping then?' asked the Swallow: 'you have quite drenched me.'

'When I was alive and had a human heart,' answered the statue, 'I did not know what tears were, for I lived in the Palace of Sans-Souci, where sorrow is not allowed to enter. In the daytime I played with my companions in the garden, and in the evening I led the dance in the Great Hall. Round the garden ran a very lofty wall, but I never cared to ask what lay beyond it, everything about me was so beautiful. My courtiers called me the Happy Prince and happy indeed I was, if pleasure be happiness. So I lived, and so I died. And now that I am dead they have set me up here so high that I can see all the ugliness and all the misery of my city, and though my heart is made of lead yet I cannot choose but weep.'

'What! is he not of solid gold?' said the Swallow to himself. He was far too polite to make any personal remarks out loud.

'Far away,' continued the statue in a low musical voice, 'far away in a little street there is a poor house. One of the windows is open, and through it I can see a woman seated at a table. Her face is thin and worn, and she has coarse, red hands, all pricked by the needle, for she is a seamstress. She is embroidering passion-flowers on a satin gown for the loveliest of the Queen's maids-of-honour to wear at the next Court ball. In a bed in the corner of the room her little boy is lying ill. He has a fever and is asking for oranges. His mother has nothing to give him but river water, so he is crying. Swallow, Swallow, little Swallow, will you not bring her the ruby out of my sword-hilt? My feet are fastened to this pedestal and I cannot move.'

'I am waited for in Egypt,' said the Swallow. 'My friends are flying up and down the Nile, and talking to the large lotus-flowers. Soon they will go to sleep in the tomb of the great King. The King is there himself in his painted coffin. He is wrapped in yellow linen, and embalmed with spices. Round his neck is a chain of pale green jade, and his hands are like withered leaves.'

'Swallow, Swallow, little Swallow,' said the Prince, 'will you not stay with me for one night, and be my messenger? The boy is so thirsty, and the mother so sad.'

'I don't think I like boys,' answered the Swallow. 'Last summer, when I was staying on the river, there were two rude boys, the miller's sons, who were always throwing stones at me. They never hit me, of course; we swallows fly far too well for that, and besides I come of a family famous for its agility; but still, it was a mark of disrespect.'

But the Happy Prince looked so sad that the little Swallow was sorry. 'It is very cold here,' he said, 'but I will stay with you for one night, and be your messenger.'

'Thank you, little Swallow,' said the Prince.

So the Swallow picked out the great ruby from the Prince's sword, and flew away with it in his beak over the roofs of the town.

He passed by the cathedral tower, where the white marble angels were sculptured. He passed by the palace and heard the sound of dancing. A beautiful girl came out on the balcony with her lover. 'How wonderful the stars are,' he said to her, 'and how wonderful is the power of love.'

'I hope my dress will be ready in time for the State ball,' she answered. 'I have ordered passion-flowers to be embroidered on it; but the seamstresses are so lazy.'

He passed over the river, and saw the lanterns hanging on the masts of the ships. At last he came to the poor house and looked in. The boy was tossing feverishly on his bed, and the mother had fallen asleep, she was so tired. In he hopped, and laid the great ruby on the table beside the woman's thimble. Then he flew gently round the bed, fanning the boy's forehead with his wings. 'How cool I feel!' said the boy, 'I must be getting better'; and he sank into a delicious slumber.

Then the Swallow flew back to the Happy Prince, and told him what he had done. 'It is curious,' he remarked, 'but I feel quite warm now, although it is so cold.'

'That is because you have done a good action,' said the Prince. And the little Swallow began to think, and then he fell asleep. Thinking always made him sleepy.

When day broke he flew down to the river and had a bath. 'What a remarkable phenomenon!' said the Professor of Ornithology as he was passing over the bridge. 'A swallow in winter!' And he wrote a long letter about it to the local newspaper. Everyone quoted it, it was so full of so many words that they could not understand.

'Tonight I go to Egypt,' said the Swallow, and he was in high spirits at the prospect. He visited all the public monuments, and sat a long time on top of the church steeple. Wherever he went the Sparrows chirruped, and said to each other, 'What a distinguished stranger!' so he enjoyed himself very much.

When the moon rose he flew back to the Happy Prince. 'Have you any commissions for Egypt?' he cried. 'I am just starting.'

'Swallow, Swallow, little Swallow,' said the Prince, 'will you not stay with me one night longer?'

'I am waited for in Egypt,' answered the Swallow. 'Tomorrow my friends will fly up to the Second Cataract. The river-horse couches there among the bulrushes, and on a great granite throne sits the God Memnon. All night long he watches the stars, and when the morning star shines he utters one cry of joy, and then he is silent. At noon the yellow lions come down to the water's edge to drink. They have eyes like green beryls, and their roar is louder than the roar of the cataract.'

'Swallow, Swallow, little Swallow,' said the Prince, 'far away across the city I see a young man in a garret. He is leaning over a desk covered with papers, and in a tumbler by his side there is a bunch of withered violets. His hair is brown and crisp and his lips are red as a pomegranate, and he has large and dreamy eyes. He is trying to finish a play for the Director of the Theatre, but he is too cold to write any more. There is no fire in the grate, and hunger has made him faint.'

'I will wait with you one night longer,' said the Swallow, who really had a good heart. 'Shall I take him another ruby?'

'Alas! I have no ruby now,' said the Prince; 'my eyes are all that I have left. They are made of rare sapphires which were brought out of India a thousand years ago. Pluck out one of them, and take it to him. He will sell it to the jeweller, and buy firewood, and finish his play.'

'Dear Prince,' said the Swallow, 'I cannot do that,' and he began to weep.

'Swallow, Swallow, little Swallow,' said the Prince, 'do as I command you.'

So the Swallow plucked out the Prince's eye, and flew away to the student's garret. It was easy enough to get in, as there was a hole in the roof. Through this he darted, and came into the room. The young man had his head buried in his hands, so he did not hear the flutter of the bird's wings, and when he looked up he found the beautiful sapphire lying on the withered violets.

'I am beginning to be appreciated,' he cried. 'This is from some great admirer. Now I can finish my play,' and he looked quite happy.

The next day the Swallow flew down to the harbour. He sat on the mast of a large vessel and watched the sailors hauling big chests out of the hold with ropes. 'Heave a-hoy!' they shouted as each chest came up.

'I am going to Egypt!' cried the Swallow, but nobody minded, and when the moon rose he flew back to the Happy Prince.

'I am come to bid you goodbye,' he cried.

'Swallow, Swallow, little Swallow,' said the Prince, 'will you not stay with me one night longer?'

'It is winter,' answered the Swallow, 'and the chill snow will soon be here. In Egypt the sun is warm on the green palm-trees, and the crocodiles lie in the mud and look lazily about them. My companions are building a nest in the Temple of Baalbec, and the pink and white doves are watching them, and cooing to each other. Dear Prince I must leave you, but I will never forget you, and next spring I will bring you back two beautiful jewels in place of those you have given away. The ruby shall be redder than a red rose, and the sapphire shall be as blue as the great sea.'

'In the square below,' said the Happy Prince, 'there stands a little match-girl. She has let her matches fall in the gutter, and they are all spoiled. Her father will beat her if she does not bring home some money, and she is crying. She has no shoes or stockings, and her little head is bare. Pluck out my other eye, and give it to her, and her father will not beat her.'

'I will stay with you one night longer,' said the Swallow, 'but I cannot pluck out your eye. You would be quite blind then.'

'Swallow, Swallow, little Swallow,' said the Prince, 'do as I command you.'

So he plucked out the Prince's other eye, and darted down with it. He swooped past the match-girl, and slipped the jewel into the palm of her hand. 'What a lovely bit of glass!' cried the little girl; and she ran home, laughing.

Then the Swallow came back to the Prince. 'You are blind now,' he said, 'so I will stay with you always.'

'No, little Swallow,' said the poor Prince, 'you must go away to Egypt.'

'I will stay with you always,' said the Swallow, and he slept at the Prince's feet.

All the next day he sat on the Prince's shoulder, and told him stories of what he had seen in strange lands. He told him of the red ibises, who stand in long rows on the banks of the Nile and catch goldfish in their beaks; of the Sphinx, who is as old as the world itself, and lives in the desert, and knows everything; of the merchants who walk slowly by the side of their camels and carry amber beads in their hands; of the King of the Mountains of the Moon, who is as black as ebony, and worships a large crystal; of the great snake that sleeps in a palm tree, and has twenty priests to feed it with honey-cakes; and of the pygmies who sail over a big lake on large flat leaves, and are always at war with the butterflies.

'Dear little Swallow,' said the Prince, 'you tell me of marvellous things, but more marvellous than anything is the suffering of men and of women. There is no Mystery so great as Misery. Fly over my city, little Swallow, and tell me what you see there.'

So the Swallow flew over the great city, and saw the rich making merry in their beautiful houses, while the beggars were sitting at the gates. He flew into dark lanes, and saw the white faces of starving children looking out listlessly at the black streets. Under the archway of a bridge two little boys were lying in one another's arms to try and keep themselves warm.

'How hungry we are!' they said.

'You must not lie here,' shouted the watchman, and they wandered out into the rain.

Then he flew back and told the Prince what he had seen.

'I am covered with fine gold,' said the Prince, 'you must take it off, leaf by leaf, and give to my poor; the living always think that gold can make them happy.'

Leaf after leaf of the fine gold the Swallow picked off, till the Happy Prince looked quite dull and grey. Leaf after leaf of the fine gold he brought to the poor, and the children's faces grew rosier and they laughed and played games in the street. 'We have bread now!' they cried.

Then the snow came, and after the snow came the frost. The streets looked as if they were made of silver, they were so bright and glistening: long icicles like crystal daggers hung down from the eaves of the houses, everybody went about in furs, and the little boys wore scarlet caps and skated on the ice.

The poor little Swallow grew colder and colder, but he would not leave the Prince, he loved him too well. He picked up crumbs outside the baker's door when the baker was not looking and tried to keep himself warm by flapping his wings.

But at last he knew that he was going to die. He had just enough strength to fly up to the Prince's shoulder once more. 'Goodbye, dear Prince,' he murmured, 'will you let me kiss your hand?'

'I am glad that you are going to Egypt at last, little Swallow,' said the Prince, 'you have stayed too long here; but you must kiss me on the lips, for I love you.'

'It is not to Egypt that I am going,' said the Swallow. 'I am going to the House of Death. Death is the brother of Sleep, is he not?'

And he kissed the Happy Prince on the lips and fell down dead at his feet. At that moment a curious crack sounded inside the statue as if something had broken. The fact is that the leaden heart had snapped right in two. It certainly was a dreadfully hard frost.

Early the next morning the Mayor was walking in the square below in company with the Town Councillors. As they passed the column he looked up at the statue: 'Dear me! how shabby the Happy Prince looks!' he said.

'How shabby, indeed,' cried the Town Councillors, who always agreed with the Mayor: and they went up to look at it.

'The ruby has fallen out of his sword, his eyes are gone, and he is golden no longer,' said the mayor, 'in fact he is little better than a beggar!'

'Little better than a beggar,' said the Town Councillors.

'And here is actually a dead bird at his feet!' continued the Mayor. 'We must really issue a proclamation that birds are not to be allowed to die here.' And the Town Clerk made a note of the suggestion.

So they pulled down the statue of the Happy Prince. 'As he is no longer beautiful he is no longer useful,' said the Art Professor at the University.

[97]

Then they melted the statue in a furnace, and the Mayor held a meeting of the Corporation to decide what was to be done with the metal.

'We must have another statue, of course,' he said, 'and it shall be a statue of myself.'

'Of myself,' said each of the Town Councillors, and they quarrelled. When I last heard of them they were quarrelling still.

'What a strange thing!' said the overseer of the workmen at the foundry. 'This broken lead heart will not melt in the furnace. We must throw it away.' So they threw in on a dust-heap where the dead Swallow was also lying.

'Bring me the two most precious things in the city,' said God to one of His Angels; and the Angel brought Him the leaden heart and the dead bird.

'You have rightly chosen,' said God, 'for in my garden of Paradise this little bird shall sing for evermore and in my city of gold the Happy Prince shall praise Me.'

Iduna and Her Golden Casket of Apples

Odin, the All-Father of the great Norse gods in ancient times, dwelt with his fellow gods and goddesses in the kingdom of Asgard.

Now it was Odin's custom to travel forth from Asgard to see how men fared in the world of Midgard below. One day, wearing his customary disguise – a faded blue cloak, a wide-brimmed hat covering his one eye (he had sacrificed the other to the giant Mimir in return for the wisdom he had drunk in at the Fountain of Knowledge), Odin set out on such a visit with his brother, Honir.

They met a handsome young man with a shock of red hair falling to his shoulders. 'Greetings to you, Odin and Honir,' he said, his eyes twinkling with mischief, for he had recognized them, disguised though Odin was. 'May I accompany you in your wanderings, for though I, Loki, am of giant blood, yet I will show you that I am worthy to join the Aesir, those great gods who dwell in the Halls of Asgard, in the fight against the giants of Jotunheim.'

Loki was a trickster, known for his cunning, which he made use of, sometimes to help himself and his companions out of a scrape, but more often for his own vicious purposes. He had the magic power of changing himself into any shape or form he wished.

Odin and Honir, now joined by Loki, wandered far and wide over deserted countryside till they were overcome with hunger. Loki was quick to track down a herd of oxen and in no time he had kindled a fire by rubbing two sticks together and had one of the oxen roasting on it. After a time, when they thought the meat was ready, Loki took it from the fire and got ready to carve but to his amazement he found the meat still completely raw. Then they put the meat to roast over the hottest part of the fire and after what seemed a goodly while Honir exclaimed, 'We are near to starving, surely the meat must now be ready for eating.' Then Loki lifted the roast from the fire but it was still no more cooked than the first time. Even Odin was at a loss to explain this odd state of affairs.

'Your meat will *never* be cooked,' boomed a jeering voice from the great tree above them, 'at least, not without my help.' They looked up and there in the branches of the tree sat a gigantic eagle. 'If you are willing to share your roasted ox with me, I will see that it gets cooked.' The hungry travellers were obliged to agree to this and the mighty bird flew down and fanned the flames with his enormous pinions. In no time the meat was roasted to perfection and the eagle greedily snatched the largest portions for himself, leaving precious little for the others.

Loki sprang up in rage. 'And what about our share,' he shouted and, grabbing the nearest branch, struck the eagle with it. The branch got stuck in the eagle's feathers as it flew upwards but Loki's hands were also stuck – to the other end of it, and the eagle pulled him aloft, dragging him over rocks and stones till Loki's body was bruised all over and his arms almost torn from their sockets. He begged the eagle to set him free, offering him the rest of the meat or any other reward he desired.

'I do not want your ox,' croaked the eagle. 'But you must make me this promise, on oath: that you will bring Iduna out of Asgard with her golden casket of the Apples of Youth. Only then will I release you and take you back to your companions.'

Now Iduna was the beautiful Earth Maiden who had but recently come to Asgard as bride to Odin's son Bragi, god of poetry and sweet music, which he played upon a golden harp. Bragi was much loved by all the Aesir and warm was their welcome to the lovely lady who carried in her hands a casket of gold in which were the Apples of Youth. To each of the gods she gave one of her apples and even as they ate it they could feel fresh blood coursing through their veins and a renewal of youth in their bodies. And however many apples she gave to the Aesir, her golden casket remained full.

Now when the eagle had asked Loki to bring Iduna out of Asgard, he had shouted in dismay, 'You are asking me to promise what is impossible. I am not even one of the Aesir, so I cannot enter Asgard.'

'Then I'll drag you from crag to rock and rock to crag until you are torn to pieces,' the eagle had threatened.

Loki in terror promised to do whatever the eagle demanded; he had to swear that he would bring Iduna to a certain wood in Midgard. Then the eagle, who was in reality the Storm Giant, Thjazi, in disguise, flew back with Loki to where the two gods were, wondering what had become of him. Loki did not tell the gods of the promise he had made and Odin suspected nothing. Indeed, he was so pleased with Loki that he provided him with a dwelling in Midgard so near to Asgard that he was separated from it only by the Bifrost Bridge (which we mortals now know as the rainbow). Loki grinned to himself. One day, he thought to himself, I too shall dwell in Asgard and the Aesir will welcome me as one of them.

And now Loki set his mischievous wits to work to lure Iduna – with her apples – out of Asgard. One day he saw her descending the Bifrost Bridge with Bragi her husband. They were taking a gentle walk in the pleasant woods and fields of Midgard. Loki, in one of his many disguises, stopped her as she strayed for a moment away from her husband to gather a few pretty flowers. 'Fair Lady Iduna,' he began, 'I have heard talk of some wondrous apples growing on a tree in a little wood nearby. Indeed, they have been likened to the magic Apples of Youth that you alone possess and for which you are justly renowned. Should we not look at these apples and compare them with your own? Then, perhaps, we might gather them to give to the Aesir.'

'There cannot anywhere be any apples like mine,' said Iduna, 'for surely to me and me alone did the great Mother Earth entrust her precious gift of the Apples of Youth. Therefore, I must indeed see for myself these apples of which you speak. Tomorrow then I shall return with my casket of apples to compare them with those in the little wood.'

Loki lost no time in informing the Giant Thjazi of the meeting place for the morrow.

The next day, in the same disguise as before, Loki waited at the foot of Bifrost till the beauteous Iduna came down the rainbow bridge. She was carrying the golden casket of apples in her hands. Loki led her into the wood, then slipped away while she had turned aside for one brief instant. At that moment the giant eagle swooped down and carried her off to his castle on the topmost peak of the rocky mountain in his kingdom of Jotunheim, where the winds howl unceasing from dawn to dark.

'You are now in my power, for no one can ever rescue you from here,' thundered Thjazi. 'If you would but give me leave to partake of your magic Apples of Youth, I will make you my Queen.'

'I will never, never be your Queen,' replied Iduna, her voice trembling, 'for I am the wife of Bragi, minstrel of the gods and my Apples are for the Aesir alone.'

'You shall be locked away in the tower at the top of my castle until you are ready to grant me what I ask,' went on Thjazi and he stormed off.

Meanwhile in Asgard Iduna was nowhere to be found. The Aesir were missing her nightly visit to the banqueting hall where she had so generously distributed her magical apples from the golden casket. Age was already creeping up on the gods and Bragi was stricken with grief; nor could he offer any explanation for her sudden disappearance. The tunes he played on his golden harp were deeply sad and he had no idea where to begin to search for his loved one.

Then Odin dispatched his two ravens – his faithful messengers, who would bring back tidings from distant lands. After many a long day they returned with news: they had indeed seen Iduna, pale and pining, sitting in the window in the topmost tower of the Storm Giant's castle, on the lone, rocky mountain in Jotunheim. In her hand she held the golden casket of apples, her voice crying out for Bragi to take her back home to Asgard where she rightly belonged.

The Aesir sat in council and Honir reminded Odin how Loki had accompanied them on their travels and had helped them when they were in trouble. Loki would now come to the rescue and win back Iduna to the home of the gods.

So Odin, Honir, Bragi and the gods went down over Bifrost Bridge to where Loki dwelt. They told him that Iduna had been stolen away and asked if he would help to get her back.

'I might be able to rescue the Lady Iduna,' he said with a cunning

little smile, 'but how am I to bring her home? I am not one of the Aesir and therefore cannot enter Asgard.'

Then Odin spoke. 'If you can bring Iduna safely to Asgard with her Apples of Youth,' he said, 'then we will make *you* one of the Aesir and you shall live with us here in Asgard as one of the gods.'

Then Loki swore an oath of loyalty to the Aesir and told them to make ready a great fire in the gateway of Asgard, but not to set it alight until they saw him approaching with Iduna, in whatever guise he chose to assume. He reminded them that the Storm Giant could only take on the form of a mighty eagle.

In no time Loki was away and as soon as he was out of sight of the Aesir, he turned himself into a falcon and flew up and up into the kingdom of Jotunheim till he came near to the castle on the high rocky mountain. He wheeled around listening for news of Thjazi's whereabouts. When he learned that he was out fishing he flew up and into the window of the castle tower where the beautiful goddess Iduna sat, her gaze ever directed towards Asgard.

'Lady Iduna,' he cried, 'I have come to rescue you and to take you back to Bragi in the kingdom of Asgard. Take with you your casket of apples and trust me whatever I do.'

'I will trust you and bless you forever,' she said.

Then Loki, the falcon, changed Iduna into a tiny nut and flew off carrying her in his talons. In a short while Thjazi returned and found that Iduna had vanished. His servants had seen no one but a falcon flying from the tower window. Then Thjazi donned his eagle plumage and with a flap of his powerful pinions swept off in hot pursuit. He tore across Jotunheim, over Midgard and was fast approaching Asgard, nearer and nearer to the flying Loki-falcon with Iduna in his talons.

The gods were watching with bated breath and suddenly Heimdall, the far-sighted one, cried, 'I see a falcon flying towards Asgard carrying something tiny, like a nut, and following in frantic chase comes Thjazi, the Storm Giant, in the guise of an eagle. Closer and ever closer comes the falcon – but look . . . the eagle is about to overtake him.'

Instantly the Aesir set fire to the wood-pile and the eagle, unable to stop in its flight, as he stretched out to grab the falcon, failed to seize it but plunged headlong into the hungry flames. Loki, of course, just skimmed the fire which he had expected would be there.

Loki now stood before the gods. He was one of them, one of the Aesir. The lovely Iduna, in her true shape, with her golden casket in her hand, embraced Bragi, her beloved husband. And the gods blessed her and were happy once again, and the Apples of Youth kept them ever young.

Niame's Gold and Silver Twins

In Africa they tell of the great god Niame, who lived up above on the Cloud Kraal. Niame had herds of cattle and a fine farm, but no one to share in his riches. He decided at last to take a wife, and the news caused a flutter among the single young ladies of the clouds, who put on their best beads and bangles, and oiled their ebony skins to a high shine, in the hope of attracting attention.

Four of the girls were so gay and pretty that Niame found it hard to choose between them. The first girl agreed to sweep out his farm and keep the house clean and tidy, if she were to become Niame's wife. The second girl offered to spin mountains of cotton, and go to the river every day for water, if Niame would marry her. The third girl, whose name was Acoco, said that she would cook perfect meals, and never complain, no matter how many unexpected guests there were for dinner.

'What more can one desire than a woman who never complains?' thought Niame, and had almost made up his mind to have Acoco for his wife, when the fourth girl spoke:

'Marry me, Niame, and I shall give you a son made of pure gold,' she said. 'And a son of silver, too.' Of course Niame saw at once he could not expect to do better than *that*, and announced his decision to marry the fourth girl.

Now Acoco, who had so nearly been chosen, was bitterly jealous, but she pretended to be pleased, as were the other two girls, with her friend's good fortune. After the wedding feast, when Niame's wife went to live on the grand farm, Acoco visited her nearly every day. Though she seemed fond of the girl, Acoco planned to do her harm, but she was obliged to bide her time while Niame was around. It would not do to incur the wrath of a god, and Niame had a fiery temper when aroused.

Within a year, Niame's wife presented him with twin sons, and the babies were just as warm and wriggly as any you have seen. But the first born was made of gold, and the second of silver. Niame was even prouder than most fathers have a right to be. He went off to drink the health of his sons, with the other gods in the Cloud Kraal, thinking his family were safe in the care of Acoco. As soon as he was gone, the scheming creature took the twins, shut them in a basket, and hid it in a hollow tree. Then she found two ugly toads and put them in the babies' bed. When Niame returned, eager to see his wonderful sons again, he saw instead the toads, staring pop-eyed at him from the cradle. The god sent for Acoco in dismay.

'What has become of my boys?' Niame demanded of her. Acoco raised her hands in mock surprise. 'Did your wife not tell you, as she told me, that the gold son and the silver son would turn into toads before they were four days old?' she asked.

'Why, it is only to be expected of gold and silver children. They are very extraordinary, after all.'

'My wife has cheated me, and I should have been better off married to one of the other girls,' groaned Niame. He threw the toads in the river, and sent his unfortunate wife, who did not know what had happened, to the darkest cloud. Acoco, satisfied with the trouble she had caused, went gleefully back home.

Although they were gold and silver, the two babies could howl with the best, and when Acoco had abandoned them in the tree, they cried dismally. A passing hunter crouched warily down in the bush, his spear poised, thinking that the noise came from some wild animal. Then he heard a creaking sound, and spotted the basket rocking wildly in the tree hollow, as the babies struggled to escape. The hunter approached and lifted the lid cautiously, for fear something unpleasant might leap up at him.

When he saw nothing more dangerous than two pairs of soft sad baby eyes, blinking away tears, the hunter opened the basket and lifted the twins out. He gasped in amazement as they shimmered and shone in the light of day. The man carried the babies home to his humble mud hut, and when he had put them to bed, he found that his hands were covered with gold and silver dust from their bodies. Next day, as the babies crawled about on the floor of the hut, they shed more and more precious dust, and the hunter swept it all up, and made himself a fortune. He was determined never to give up so valuable a pair of babies, no matter to whom they really belonged, though he knew well enough they must belong to someone. This was not honest, but, to give him his due, the hunter took great care of the babies, and treated them most kindly. Six years passed and the twins thrived. They grew into a pair of fine lively lads. The hunter had become so rich that his house was inlaid with gold and silver, and the dazzling sight could be seen miles away on a clear day. Niame himself happened to catch its reflection in a shaft of sunlight, and followed the bright path until he came to the hunter's house. The hunter was sitting outside, with the gold and silver twins.

'Where did you find those beautiful children?' Niame asked. 'They resemble closely some sons of mine who, unhappily, turned into toads.' The hunter guessed that Niame must be the father of his treasures, but he did not intend to part with them. 'These are no toads, but the children of my mother's own sister's daughter,' he replied untruthfully.

'But these boys are gold and silver,' observed Niame. 'Only a god may have such children.' The hunter, however, said that he was quite mistaken.

'It is the strong morning sun that shines upon the skin of this boy, making him only appear to be gold,' he explained.

'And what of the silver boy?' Niame persisted. 'He is surely a son of mine.'

'It is the cold light that comes from the northern hills which shines upon the skin of this boy, making him only appear to be silver,' said the crafty hunter. Niame began to walk away, crestfallen, when suddenly he saw that the ground was covered with small gold and silver footprints. Stooping, he touched some of the prints, and his fingers came away tipped with pure gold and silver dust. Niame knew then that the twins were indeed his own long-lost sons, and the hunter saw the game was up. The twins were handed over to Niame, who would have punished the hunter as he deserved, but for the golden boy. He had a heart of gold, and begged his father to forgive the man, because he had treated them well. Even then Niame hardly looked pleased, and it was not until the silver boy stood on his hands, and walked about comically, that he smilingly relented and forgave the hunter. The boy had a quicksilver temperament, and could make anyone feel merry.

When Niame had taken his sons home, he sent for Acoco. Finding the children alive and well, she broke down and confessed her wickedness. Niame, learning that the pretty face only served to hide an ugly nature, turned Acoco into a hideous snake, so that everyone should see at once how nasty she was. Then the god sent for his wife, and in order to make up for such unfair treatment, gave her a new serving woman, who was as devoted as Acoco had been treacherous.

It is said that the twins bathe in a great river that flows from the clouds, and that their precious dust is washed down to us. True or false, gold has certainly been found in many a river on earth, and this is hard to account for.

The Crock of Gold

There was once a farmer's son, Tom Fitzpatrick, as fine and upstanding a young fellow as you'd find anywhere in Ireland. It was a holiday and there was a dance at the crossroads. Tom knew that the prettiest girls in the countryside would be there, so he put on his Sunday clothes and set out to join them.

As he walked round the edge of a field, he heard a sharp little click in the hedge. Sure and it's too late for a stone-chat? he thought and stopped to look amongst the bushes.

There in a hollow amongst the ripe blackberries was a tiny man only the height of your knee, sitting on a three-legged stool and hammering heels on a pair of shoes with silver buckles. Tom didn't need to be told who the little man was, for every Irishman knows a Leprechaun when he sees one and knows too that a Leprechaun has a crock of gold hidden away somewhere.

'God bless the work,' he said.

'Thank you kindly,' said the Leprechaun.

'It's is a wonder to see you working and it being a holiday,' said Tom.

'That's as it may be,' said the Leprechaun and he took a drink from a little pitcher beside him.

'It's dry work making shoes,' said Tom.

'It is that same,' said the Leprechaun.

'What might it be in the pitcher?' asked Tom.

'Good Irish beer,' said the little man.

'Where did you get that?' asked Tom.

'I brewed it myself,' said the Leprechaun, looking at Tom over the top of the pitcher.

'Will you give me a taste of it?' asked Tom and he came a little nearer.

'Look to your father's corn!' said the Leprechaun quickly. 'It's destroyed it will be if you don't drive away the cows.'

Tom jumped and was just about to turn round when he remembered the ways of leprechauns. Take your eye off them and they whip out of sight. 'You'll not catch me out that way!' he said and grabbed the little fellow by the tail of his green coat.

'Now,' he said very fiercely, 'take me to your crock of gold, wherever it is you have hidden it, or I'll not be letting you go this side of Christmas.'

The Leprechaun was frightened. He swore he had no crock of gold, but Tom wasn't to be put off by that. The little man twisted and turned and tried all the tricks he knew to make Tom look elsewhere, but it was all no good. Tom was determined not to let him go, for a crock of gold he would have. Why, he could buy that plot of land near his father's fields and marry pretty Molly Maloney! He shook the Leprechaun until he cried out for mercy and at last gave in.

'Bad luck to you, I'll show you where I've hidden my gold,' he said. 'It's not very far away, but I warn you it's rough walking. I fear it'll be hard on your Sunday clothes.'

Tom all but looked down at his clothes, but, just in time, he remembered not to take his eyes off the Leprechaun.

'Lead the way and no more havering,' he said as fiercely as he could. Off went the little man and Tom after him, his eyes fixed on the fellow's back. Small as he was, the Leprechaun could keep up a good pace and he led Tom through every thorn bush and scraped him through every hedge and splashed him through every boggy patch, until Tom's best clothes weren't fit to be seen. But never once did he take his eyes off the Leprechaun.

'We're near it now,' said the Leprechaun at last. They had come out into the twenty-acre field. It was full of fine yellow ragwort which glowed fierily in the sunset. The Leprechaun walked a little way into it and stopped under a ragwort plant about twice the height of himself. There he stood in his green coat and said, 'Dig under this, and you'll find my own crock of gold. It's well dug in so it's a pity you haven't a spade.'

'That'll not be bothering me,' said Tom. 'I'll soon get one.' He thought of the field of yellow ragwort stretching so far around him. But how shall I know which plant to dig under when I come back? he wondered. Sure, I must mark the right one somehow.

After much thought he took off his red knitted garter from his leg and tied it round the stem of the ragwort under which the Leprechaun had hidden his crock of gold – so he said.

'You have a head on you,' said the Leprechaun admiringly. 'Is that all you'll be wanting of me?'

'Thank you kindly,' said Tom as politely as you please now he'd got his own way. 'God speed you.'

'That's as it may be,' said the Leprechaun, 'but you're welcome to what you find,' and he disappeared amongst the ragwort. One moment he was there, the next he was not.

Tom set off as fast as he could for home. He didn't wait to change his Sunday suit – after all when he was rich with the Leprechaun's gold, he could buy as many new clothes as he liked. He caught up a spade and hurried back to the twenty-acre field. The field faced the sunset and he was fairly dazzled with the light of it in his eyes. I've never seen it look so red, thought Tom and he began to search for his red garter. That was soon done for every single ragwort in the field was tied round with a red garter the like of his own!

Tom stood and stared. 'And what will I be doing now?' he said indignantly. 'It's the whole field I'd have to dig. All twenty acres of it!'

Well, Tom knew that he'd never do that in a year. 'Bad luck to you wherever you are!' he shouted to the Leprechaun, but the little man, wherever he was, lay low and made no answer.

Away went Tom back to the farm, feeling very sorry for himself, his clothes in such rags that he couldn't for very shame show himself at the dance.

And although he looked for a Leprechaun many times, he never set eyes on one again, nor on a crock of gold.

The Prince with the Golden Hand

Once there lived a King and Queen who had an only daughter. Her hair was golden, hanging to her waist. She was of such dazzling beauty that princes from far and wide were vying with each other to win her. They had seen only her picture, as for sixteen years the Princess had lived in her own rooms. She never saw anyone but her parents, the King and Queen, her teachers and her servants. She never went anywhere and never looked upon the outside world nor breathed the outer air.

But on her eighteenth birthday she happened by chance to hear the cry of the cuckoo and this sound made her feel curiously uneasy. She covered her eyes with her hands and fell into deep thought. Then an irresistible longing to walk in the free air in the gardens she had so long looked at through the lattice windows took hold of her. She persuaded her governesses to throw open the doors and promised to keep close by them.

The Princess was overwhelmed by the sweet scent of the flowers and she ran about picking them and chasing the multi-coloured butterflies. One moment she was there, laughing happily, but the next a raging hurricane swept the earth, seizing the Princess and carrying her far away. The terrified governesses were struck dumb in despair. In vain they searched everywhere for the Princess and the King and Queen were left in a state of deepest grief. Their great sorrow soon became known abroad and a royal proclamation by the King announced that the Princess, when found, would be the bride of the one who brought her back safe from the Kingdom of Vikher, the Hurricane Giant who had taken her prisoner.

Among the many princes who came as suitors were two royal brothers. They journeyed together through many a land asking everyone they met if they had seen the princess with the long golden tresses. But no one had seen her. At last they arrived at a country which lies in the centre of the earth and where, strangely, summer and winter seasons fall at the same time. They came to a lofty mountain, left their horses to graze in the valley and then began their climb. When they reached the summit, they came face to face with a magnificent silver palace perched precariously on a craggy rock and at one of its windows they espied a beautiful lady whose golden hair shone in the sun. But suddenly a winter wind blew so fiercely and with such intense cold that the princes could not hold their footing. Their breath froze as they battled valiantly against the storm, but they were overcome by its power and fell headlong down the mountain-side and froze to death.

In vain did their parents await their return, but they would not give up hope. One day the Queen happened to be giving alms to a poor old man and she asked him to pray for her dear lost sons. 'We can only pray for everlasting peace for your dear sons, good lady,' said the man, 'for they are surely dead. But I am the bearer of better tidings, dear Queen, for the time is soon to come when you will bear a son whose like the world has yet to see.' The old man, having spoken thus, vanished.

With a strange sense of joy the Queen told the King of the old man's words and so it befell that soon a baby prince was born to her and he was indeed an extraordinary child. His right hand was of pure gold. When he was but a few days old be abandoned his baby clothes and left his cradle. His manner and bearing as he grew up were so majestic that he was looked upon by everyone with awe and love.

Yet behind his parents' love for him the Prince sensed a hidden sadness and one day he asked them to tell him of their sorrow.

'We grieve', they said, 'for your two brothers who died before you were born. They are in some strange country, not even buried in the land of their forefathers. It is some years now since we heard news of them.' At these words the son wept and fell at their feet.

'You will soon be comforted, my dear parents,' said the Prince, 'I will set forth to look for my brothers all the world over till I find them, dead or alive, and will bring them back to the land of their fathers.'

The Prince grew hour by hour and in no time he had become a handsome valiant youth. His moustache was of fine gold. Then one day he put on a helmet, mounted his horse and with his sword by his side begged his parents' blessing. 'I shall now venture to the very ends of the earth,' he said, 'to find my brothers.' His parents protested that he was still too young for such an adventure, but the young Prince replied, 'These dangers hold no fear for me. Whatever Fate has in store for us *will* happen and nothing can prevent it.'

So the King and Queen gave him their blessing and with tears in their eyes bade their son farewell.

The young Prince crossed swirling rivers, climbed high mountains and rode his horse over swampy marshland. After days of journeying he came upon a cottage in the middle of a dark forest. The strange cottage walked on hens' legs, turning this way and that with the wind. He rode up to it and called out.

> *Little cottage, turn around, open your door to me.*
> *I know old Yaga sits within, 'tis her I've come to see.*

The cottage turned, the door opened and the Prince went in. Old Yaga was truly frightful to look upon: her face was withered and wrinkled and her thin white hair hung down unkempt. Two beautiful young girls were doing the witch's bidding, sweeping and scrubbing and working very hard. She herself sat at a table with a faraway look in her mysterious eyes. 'And what has brought you here, Prince of the Golden Hand and Moustache of Gold. Your two brothers froze to death on the cloud-capped mountain as they searched for the golden-haired Princess who was carried off by Vikher the Hurricane Giant.'

'And how can I capture this villainous Vikher?' asked the Prince.

'Ah, young man, I myself, for the last hundred years, have feared to go outside this cottage lest Vikher should carry me off to his palace. He will eat you up like an insect.'

'My golden hand can smash anything,' replied the Prince, 'so I have no fear on that or any other score.'

'Then I will help you,' said old Yaga, 'but you must promise me

that you will bring me back some of the Water of Youth, for it may restore to me my girlhood freshness.'

'On that you have my word,' replied the Prince.

Then old Yaga gave him a pin-cushion and told him to throw it in front of him and follow it wherever it went. 'It will lead you to the mountain that touches the clouds,' she said. 'Perched high on a rock is Vikher's Silver Palace guarded by his father, the Northern Blast, and his mother, the South Wind. If you are attacked by the father, you will be seized with sudden cold and you will freeze to death as did your brothers; but put on this heat-giving hood and you will survive. If the South Wind tries to overpower you with her burning heat, then drink from this cooling flagon. Then follow the pin-cushion to the top of the mountain peak and into the palace.'

The young Prince took the pin-cushion, the heat-giving hood and the cooling flagon, thanked Old Yaga and mounted his steed. The pin-cushion rolled before him at a great speed as he rode off.

Now a good story is soon told, but things do not happen quite so quickly. When the Prince had travelled through many a kingdom he came at last to a beautiful valley and above it towered the mountain that touches the clouds. The summit was so high it seemed to reach the sky.

The Prince left his horse to graze and began following the pin-cushion up the steep mountain paths. When he had climbed to the top where the Silver Palace of the Hurricane Giant was shimmering on the rocky crag, the Northern Blast began to blow and the cold wind was so intense that his breath froze. He just managed to put on the heat-giving hood before it was too late. The Northern Blast blew with redoubled fury, but to no avail for the Prince was so hot under the hood that he streamed with perspiration.

Then the Prince threw the pin-cushion and it stopped on a snow-covered mound. He cleared the snow away and there he found the two frozen bodies of his brothers who had perished in their attempt to rescue the Princess with the Golden Hair. He knelt beside them and offered up a prayer.

Then the pin-cushion rolled ever higher up the rocky crag to the very topmost peak where a Silver Palace gleamed in the sun. The Princess's head, crowned with golden tresses, could be seen at one of the windows. The Prince made a sudden rush to reach the palace but a wind coming from the south attacked him so that he was all but overcome with its intense heat. He grabbed the cooling flagon from his pocket and drank deeply from it. Then he continued his ascent till he came face to face with the palace. It was a sight to wonder at, built entirely of silver with a roof of solid gold.

The Princess at the window had seen him and her eyes lit up. The Prince rushed boldly through the palace doors and found the room where the Princess was. The walls and floors consisted of mirrors so instead of one Princess he saw twelve, all of course equally beautiful with the same golden hair. But eleven were simply reflections of the one real Princess.

She gave a cry of joy on seeing him but her expression quickly changed to one of great fear. 'Whoever you are and wherever you have come from, you have surely come to deliver me from my imprisonment, but Vikher the Hurricane Giant is invincible. He will kill you with a mere glance of his eyes. You must flee before his return which I expect at any moment now.'

'If I do not succeed in saving you, dear Princess, then I do not wish to go on living. But have no fear, I will overcome the monster with your help. But first, pray let me drink of the strength-giving water from the well which Vikher imbibes daily.'

The Princess drew a bucketful of water from the well which the Prince drank at one draught and then asked for another and this, too, he swallowed at a draught. Then the Princess gave him an iron chair to rest on, but it broke into a thousand pieces when he sat on it. She then brought him the chair used by Vikher himself; although it was made of solid steel it cracked beneath the Prince's weight.

'You will see, sweet Princess, I am now heavier than your unconquerable Vikher and I shall overcome him. Now what has happened since the Hurricane Giant snatched you from your home and how do you pass your time here?' he asked.

'Alas,' she said, 'I spend my time weeping over my sad situation. Vikher the Hurricane is determined to marry me, but for two years I have kept my persecutor at bay and have withheld my consent till he can guess the riddles which I have set him. But the last time he went away he told me that when he returns he will marry me even if he has *not* guessed the riddles.'

'Then I am just in time,' said the Prince, 'he shall have *Death* for his bride.'

At that moment a whistling screech was heard. 'Here he comes,' shrieked the Princess in terror.

The Palace spun round and round and the doors opened with tremendous bangs. Vikher, on his winged horse that breathed fire from its nostrils, leapt into the room. He had the body of a giant and the head of a dragon.

'What are you doing here, stranger?' roared the giant. 'I will crush every bone in your body if you do not leave this instant.'

'Try if you dare,' retorted the Prince and he just stepped lightly aside as Vikher threw himself at him with mouth agape to swallow him. The Prince boldly plunged his Golden Hand down the monster's throat and seizing him by the tongue dashed him against the wall. Vikher crashed to the floor lifeless in a pool of blood.

The Prince then drew from the different springs The Water of Life and The Water of Youth and mounted the winged horse with the Princess in his arms.

> Winged steed of magical force
> Bear us away o'er heath and gorse,
> That we may yet our parents see
> And live for ever happily.

The horse soared upwards only to land on the exact spot where the two Princes lay in seeming frozen death. With his Golden Hand the Prince sprinkled the life-restoring water on their bodies and at once the pallor of death vanished. They opened their eyes and declared they had slept soundly. Then they recognized the Princess with the Golden Hair, for they had long gazed at her picture and had they not almost forfeited their lives in search of her? But the Prince with the Golden Hand they had never met, nor did they know, till he told his story, that he was their very own brother.

Then the brothers embraced each other and the two brothers mounted the magical steed with the Prince and Princess. The winged horse flew high up into the air and descended, at the Prince's bidding, close by the cottage of Old Yaga. She was on the look-out and came to meet them.

As soon as she sprinkled herself with the Water of Youth she was transformed into a charming maiden. And she was so happy that she was ready to do anything the Prince asked. So, at his request, the two beautiful girls, who were her prisoners for life, were set free to go wherever they pleased. The two revived Princes were happy enough to be alive once more, but when these two ladies accepted their proposals of marriage, their happiness knew no bounds. They placed their brides before them and now there were six on the back of the enchanted horse. Up he rose, flapping his wings, and flew high above the forest. In less than no time he was floating down and landed his riders in front of the Palace of the Princess with the Golden Hair.

The King and Queen, who had all but given up their daughter as lost, were overcome with joy and when they had heard the story of all their adventures they gave thanks and blessings to one and all.

'You, dear Prince with the Golden Hand, shall receive our beloved daughter in marriage and half of our kingdom besides and we rejoice in the happiness of your brothers who have found their brides in these strange adventures.'

Then the Princess with the Golden Hair spoke. 'I shall be the happiest of all beings in this world if the Prince with the Golden Hand takes me as a bride, but before I can give my consent to this betrothal, I must fulfil the vow I made when carried off by Vikher the Hurricane Giant that I would only marry the man who could give the right answer to my three riddles. I dare not and could not break my word.'

Then the Prince boldly accepted the challenge. 'Speak, sweet Princess,' he said, 'I am ready to solve them.'

Amid silence she said, 'Here is my first riddle: Two of my extremities form a sharp point at one end and two rings at the other; in my centre is a screw. What am I?'

'A pair of scissors,' replied the Prince promptly.

She smiled assent and went on to the second: 'I stand on the table on one foot, but if I should fall I am damaged beyond repair.'

'A wine glass,' said the Prince without hesitation.

'The last', said the Princess, 'is, I fear, the most difficult. I existed before the creation of Adam. I am always changing in succession the two colours of my dress, yet after thousands of years the colours remain the same.'

'The answer to that must be Time and the unchanging colours are of night and day,' replied the Prince after just a slight pause.

Then the Princess danced with delight. 'You have guessed them all.' And she offered her hand to the young Prince. They knelt before the King and Queen to receive their blessings.

Then the three Princes with their three brides mounted the winged horse who flew with them to the parents of the Princes. It would have been enough for the old King and Queen to see their youngest son, the Prince with the Golden Hand, alive and well but to find their other two sons, restored to life and each of their sons with a beautiful bride, was beyond their wildest dreams.

Meanwhile, at the Palace of the Princess of the Golden Hair, a magnificent feast was prepared. The three weddings were celebrated that same day and all their friends and families were invited. They danced and drank and feasted till the next morning. I was there so I know this story to be true.

The Three Golden Heads of the Well

L ong ago there lived a widowed King and his only daughter. She was beautiful and kind and everybody loved her. Happy she was until the King took it into his head to marry again. His new Queen had a daughter of her own and she was ill-natured and thoroughly unpleasant so that nobody liked her at all.

The new Queen was jealous of the King's daughter and was determined to get rid of her. So, handing her some dry crusts of bread and a tiny bottle of stale beer, she said, 'Go to the Well at the World's End and bring me home this bucket full of water from it.' The Queen was sure the girl would never find the well and even if she did she could never get the bucket filled, for it was riddled with tiny holes.

The young princess wandered off with a heavy heart. She had no idea which way she ought to go. She asked everyone she met if they knew of the Well at the World's End, but nobody did. At last she met a little old man all bent and hobbling on a stick and sure enough he told the girl just where to go. 'By the way, my child,' he asked, 'what's that you've got in your bag?'

'It's not much, only a few dry crusts and some stale beer,' she said, 'but I'd be happy enough to share it with you.'

The old man accepted gratefully. 'And what are you going to the

Well at the World's End for?' he asked. And the girl told him of the task she must perform and how the bucket she carried was full of holes.

'Never you fear, child, your bucket will be filled,' he said.

> Stuff it with moss and line it with clay
> And then it will carry the water away.

But the way to the well is hard, dear maiden. Look out for a pony tethered to a tree and he will help you.'

On and on she went till she came upon the pony, tethered, just as the old man had said. And the pony said to her.

> Loosen my tether and free me, I pray.
> For I've not been untied for seven years and a day.

So the girl untied his tether and the pony said, 'Jump on my back and I'll carry you across the sharp thorns of the moor.' So the girl jumped on his back and he carried her over the moor and left her just by the Well at the World's End and she had not felt the sharp thorns at all. Then she carefully lined the bucket with moss and covered the moss with earth just as the old man had told her to and sat down on the brink of the well to dip it in and fill it with water.

At that moment a scaly golden head of a man rose up from the deep well. And the head spoke to her.

> Wash me and comb me and leave me to dry,
> that I may look handsome to all passers by.

The young princess did just as she was asked and gently laid the head on the bank to dry. Then a second golden head came up singing:

> Wash me and dry me and comb out my hair
> That I may look goodly and comely and fair.

'Gladly will I do that,' she said, and she combed out his hair so that it shone bright in the sun.

Then a third head of gold appeared.

'Oh pray wash my head O bonny kind maid, and then put me back,' was all that he said. And the maid did just as she was bid with the sweetest goodwill.

Then the three gold heads talked things over. 'What shall we wish for this bonny maid who had been so kind to us?'

The first head said, 'I wish that if she was bonny before she'll be ten times bonnier now.'

'I wish', said the second head, 'that every time she speaks a diamond, a ruby and a pearl will drop from her lips.'

And the third head wished that each time she combed her hair a peck of gold and silver would fall from her comb.

Then the three heads filled her bucket with water from the well and the King's daughter wished herself home.

The pony appeared and carried her straight away through the moor of sharp thorns and the bucket she held carefully in her hand and not a single drop of water did she spill.

When the Queen saw her she went purple with anger. The girl looked even bonnier than before. Each time she spoke a diamond, a ruby and a pearl dropped from her lips and when she combed her hair a shower of gold and silver fell from the comb.

So the Queen sent her own daughter to the Well of the World's End, hoping she would meet with the same good fortune. She gave her a bottle to fill at the Well and some cakes and fine bread to eat and some honeyed milk to drink.

The girl soon came upon the little old man all bent and hobbling on a stick. She asked him if he knew where the Well at the World's End was and he told her the way was hard but perhaps the pony on the moors, tethered to a tree might help her to get there. And he caught a whiff of good food to eat in her bag.

'And what have you got in that bag that smells so good and delicious?' he asked.

'What's it to do with you?' she snapped, and as if to spite him she sat down right in front of him to enjoy her goodies and not one scrap did she offer to share.

The Queen's daughter went on and on till she came upon the pony tethered to the tree.

Loosen my tether, young maiden, I pray
For I long to be free and ride far away.

'Stop bothering me, you stupid creature,' she cried, 'I am the Queen's daughter with other things to worry about.'

'Then I'll not carry you over the moor of sharp thorns,' said the pony.

So the Queen's daughter had to cross the moor on foot and the

sharp thorns scratched her all over so that she could hardly walk at all. At long last she came to the Well at the World's End. She sat on the brink wondering how she was to reach the water so deep down to fill her bottle.

Suddenly there rose up from the deep well the scaly golden head of a man; then came a second head and yet a third followed. All three of then started singing:

> Wash us and comb us and leave us to dry
> So we may look comely to all passers by.

'Get back down into the well, you horrid creatures,' she cried. 'Why, I am a Queen's daughter; fancy asking me to wash you.' And she poked and pushed them rudely with her glass bottle.

Then the three golden heads got together and conferred. 'What shall we wish her, this ill-mannered girl?' they asked each other.

The first head said, 'I wish that if she was ugly before, she'll be ten times uglier now.'

'I', said the second, 'wish that every time she speaks a toad will drop from her mouth.'

'And I', said the third head, 'wish that every time she combs her hair a swarm of fleas will fall from it.'

Then the three golden heads disappeared into the well.

So the Queen's daughter had to return with an empty bottle. Once more she had to cross the thorny moors on foot.

When the Queen saw her face ten times uglier than it was before and saw a toad fall from her mouth each time she spoke and a swarm of fleas fall from her hair when she combed it she drove the girl away from the court. But when the King heard how the Queen had ill-treated *his* daughter, the Queen, too, was driven out, never to return.

A noble young prince married the King's daughter, as kind and as handsome as she was sweet-natured and beautiful. Diamonds, pearls and rubies were theirs for the asking.

As for the daughter of the Queen, she had to put up with a husband as ill-natured as herself and which of the pair got the better of things we never shall know.

The Maid with Hair of Gold

There was once a king so wise and clever that he understood the language of all animals. You shall hear how he gained this power.

One day an old woman came to the palace and said, 'I wish to speak to His Majesty, for I have something of great importance to tell him.' When admitted to his presence she presented him with a curious fish, saying, 'Have it cooked for yourself, and when you have eaten it you will understand all that is said by the birds of the air, the animals that walk the earth, and the fishes that live under the waters.'

The king was delighted to know that which every one else was ignorant of, so he rewarded the old woman generously, and told a servant to cook the fish very carefully.

'But take care', said the monarch, 'that you do not taste it yourself, for if you do you will be killed.'

Georgy, the servant, was astonished at such a threat, and wondered why his master was so anxious that no one else should eat any of the fish. Then examining it curiously he said, 'Never in all my life have I seen such an odd-looking fish; it seems more like a reptile. Now where would be the harm if I did take some? Every cook tastes of the dishes he prepares.'

When it was fried he tasted a small piece, and while taking some of the sauce he heard a buzzing in the air and a voice speaking in his ear.

'Let us taste a crumb: let us taste a little,' it said.

He looked round to see where the words came from, but there were only a few flies buzzing about in the kitchen. At the same moment someone out in the yard said in a harsh jerky voice, 'Where are we going to settle? Where?'

And another answered, 'In the miller's barley field; ho! for the miller's field of barley.'

When Georgy looked towards where this strange talk came he saw a gander flying at the head of a flock of geese.

'How lucky,' thought he; 'now I know why my master set so much value on this fish and wished to eat it all himself.'

Georgy had now no doubt that by tasting the fish he had learnt the language of animals, so after having taken a little more he served the king with the remainder as if nothing had happened.

When his majesty had dined he ordered Georgy to saddle two horses and accompany him for a ride. They were soon off, the master in front, the servant behind.

While crossing a meadow Georgy's horse began to prance and caper, neighing out these words, 'I say, brother, I feel so light and in such good spirits today that in one single bound I could leap over those mountains yonder.'

'I could do the same,' answered the king's horse, 'but I carry a feeble old man on my back; he would fall like a log and break his skull.'

'What does that matter to you? So much the better if he should break his head, for then, instead of being ridden by an old man you would probably be mounted by a young one.'

The servant laughed a good deal upon hearing this conversation between the horses, but he took care to do so on the quiet, lest the king should hear him. At that moment His Majesty turned round, and, seeing a smile on the man's face, asked the cause of it.

'Oh nothing, Your Majesty, only some nonsense that came into my head.'

The king said nothing, and asked no more questions, but he was suspicious, and distrusted both servant and horses; so he hastened back to the palace.

When there he said to Georgy, 'Give me some wine, but mind you only pour out enough to fill the glass, for if you put in one drop too much, so that it overflows, I shall certainly order my executioner to cut off your head.'

While he was speaking two birds flew near the window, one chasing the other, who carried three golden hairs in his beak.

'Give them to me,' said one, 'you know they are mine.'

'Not at all, I picked them up myself.'

'No matter, I saw them fall while the Maid with Hair of Gold was combing out her hair. At least, give me two, then you can keep the third for yourself.'

'No not a single one.'

Thereupon one of the birds succeeded in seizing the hairs from the other bird's beak, but in the struggle he let one fall, and it made a sound as if a piece of metal had struck the ground. As for Georgy, he was completely taken off his guard, and the wine overflowed the glass.

The king was furious, and feeling convinced that his servant had disobeyed him and had learnt the language of animals, he said, 'You scoundrel, you deserve death for having failed to do my bidding; nevertheless, I will show you mercy upon one condition, that you bring me the Maid with Hair of Gold, for I intend to marry her.'

Alas, what was to be done? Poor fellow, he was willing to do anything to save his life, even run the risk of losing it on a long journey. He therefore promised to search for the Maid with Hair of Gold; but he knew not where or how to find her.

When he had saddled and mounted his horse he allowed it to go its own way, and it carried him to the outskirts of a dark forest, where some shepherds had left a bush burning. The sparks of fire from the bush endangered the lives of a large number of ants which had built their nest close by, and the poor little things were hurrying away in all directions, carrying their small white eggs with them.

'Help us in our distress, good Georgy,' they cried in a plaintive voice; 'do not leave us to perish, together with our children whom we carry in these eggs.'

Georgy immediately dismounted, cut down the bush and put out the fire.

'Thank you, brave man. And remember, when you are in trouble you have only to call upon us, and we'll help you in our turn.' The young fellow went on his way far into the forest until he came to a

[129]

very tall fir tree. At the top of the tree was a raven's nest, while at the foot, on the ground, lay two young ones who were calling out to their parents and saying, 'Alas, father and mother, where have you gone? You have flown away, and we have to seek our food, weak and helpless as we are. Our wings are as yet without feathers, how then shall we be able to get anything to eat? Good Georgy,' said they, turning to the young man, 'do not leave us to starve.'

Without stopping to think, the young man dismounted, and gave all the morsels of food he had prepared for his journey to the young birds. They thanked him heartily, and said, 'If ever you should be in distress, call to us and we will help you at once.'

After this Georgy rode on, ever getting further and further into the forest. On reaching the end of it, he saw stretching before him an immense sea that seemed to mingle with the horizon. Close by stood two men disputing the possession of a large fish with golden scales that had fallen into their net.

'The net belongs to me,' said one, 'therefore the fish must be mine.'

'Your net would not have been of the slightest use, for it would have been lost in the sea, had I not come with my boat just in the nick of time.'

'Well, you shall have the next haul I make.'

'And suppose you should catch nothing? No; give me this one and keep the next haul for yourself.'

'I am going to put an end to your quarrel,' said Georgy, addressing them. 'Sell me the fish: I will pay you well, and you can divide the money between you.'

Thereupon he dismounted and put into their hands all the money the king had given him for the journey, without keeping a single coin for himself. The fishermen rejoiced at the good fortune which had befallen them, but Georgy put the fish back into the water. The fish, thankful for this unexpected freedom, dived and disappeared but, returning to the surface, said, 'Whenever you may need my help you have but to call me, I shall not fail to show my gratitude.'

'Where are you going?' asked the fishermen.

'I am in search of a wife for my old master; she is known as the Maid with Hair of Gold: but I am at a loss where to find her.'

'If that be all, we can easily give you information,' answered they. 'She is Princess Zlato Vlaska, and daughter of the king whose crystal palace is built on that island yonder. The golden light from the princess's hair is reflected on sea and sky every morning when she combs it. If you would like to go to the island we will take you there for nothing, in return for the clever and generous way by which you made us stop quarrelling. But beware of one thing: when in the palace do not make a mistake as to which is the princess, for there are twelve of them, but only Zlato Vlaska has hair of gold. So tether your horse and come with us.'

When Georgy reached the island he lost no time in making his way to the palace, and demanded from the king the hand of his daughter, Princess Zlato Valska, in marriage to the king his master.

'I will grant the request with pleasure,' said His Majesty, 'but only one one condition, namely, that you perform certain tasks which I will set you. These will be three in number, and must be done in three days, just as I order you. For the present you had better rest and refresh yourself after your journey.'

On the next day the king said, 'My daughter, the Maid with Hair of Gold, had a string of fine pearls, and the thread having broken, the pearls were scattered far and wide among the long grass of this field. Go and pick up every one of the pearls, for they must all be found.'

Georgy went into the meadow, which was of great length and stretched away far out of sight. He went down on his knees and hunted between the tufts of grass and bramble from morning until noon, but not a single pearl could he find.

'Ah, if I only had my good little ants here,' he cried, 'they would be able to help me.'

'Here we are, young man, at your service,' answered the ants, suddenly appearing. Then they all ran round him, crying out, 'What is the matter? What do you want?'

'I have to find all the pearls lost in this field, and cannot see a single one: can you help me?'

'Wait a little, we will soon get them for you.'

He had not to wait very long, for they brought him a heap of pearls, and all he had to do was to thread them on the string. Just as he was about to make a knot he saw a lame ant coming slowly towards him, for one of her feet had been burned in the bush fire.

'Wait a moment, Georgy,' she called out; 'do not tie the knot before threading this last pearl I am bringing you.'

When Georgy took his pearls to the king, his majesty first counted them to make sure they were all there, and then said, 'You have done very well in this test, tomorrow I will give you another.'

Early next morning the king summoned Georgy to him and said, 'My daughter, the Maid with Hair of Gold dropped her gold ring into the sea while bathing. You must find the jewel and bring it me today.'

The young fellow walked thoughtfully up and down the beach. The water was pure and transparent, but he could not see beyond a certain distance into its depths, and therefore could not tell where the ring was lying beneath the water.

'Ah, my golden fishling, why are you not here now? You would surely be able to help me,' he said to himself, speaking aloud.

'Here I am,' answered the fish's voice from the sea, 'what can I do for you?'

'I have to find a gold ring which has been dropped in the sea, but as I cannot see to the bottom there is no use looking.'

The fish said, 'Fortunately I have just met a pike, wearing a gold ring on his fin. Just wait a moment, will you?'

In a very short time he reappeared with the pike and the ring. The pike willingly gave up the jewel.

The king thanked Georgy for his cleverness, and then told him the third task. 'If you really wish me to give the hand of my daughter with the golden hair to the monarch who has sent you here, you must bring me two things that I want above everything: the Water of Death and the Water of Life.'

Georgy had not the least idea where to find these waters, so he determined to trust to chance and 'follow his nose', as the saying is. He went first in one direction and then in another, until he reached a dark forest.

'Ah, if my little ravens were but here, perhaps they would help me,' he said aloud.

Suddenly there was heard a rushing noise, as of wings overhead, and then down came the ravens calling 'Kraak, kraak, here we are, ready and willing to help you. What are you looking for?'

'I want some of the Water of Death and the Water of Life: it is impossible for me to find them, for I don't know where to look.'

'Kraak, kraak, we know very well where to find some. Wait a moment.'

Off they went immediately, but soon returned, each with a small gourd in his beak. One gourd contained the Water of Life, the other the Water of Death.

Georgy was delighted with his success, and went back on his way to the palace. When nearly out of the forest, he saw a spider's web hanging between two fir trees, while in the centre was a large spider devouring a fly he had just killed. Georgy sprinkled a few drops of the Water of Death on the spider; it immediately left the fly, which rolled to the ground like a ripe cherry, but on being touched with the Water of Life she began to move, and stretching out first one limb and then another, gradually freed herself from the spider's web. Then she spread her wings and took flight, having first buzzed these words in the ears of her deliverer: 'Georgy, you have assured your own happiness by restoring mine, for without my help you would never have succeeded in recognizing the Maid with Hair of Gold when you choose her tomorrow from among the twelve sisters.'

And the fly was right, for though the king, on finding that Georgy had accomplished the third task, agreed to give him his daughter Zlato Vlaska, he yet added that he would have to find her himself.

He then led him to a large room and bade him choose from among the twelve charming girls who sat at a round table. Each wore a kind of linen headdress that completely hid the upper part of the head, and in such a way that the keenest eye could not discover the colour of the hair.

'Here are my daughters,' said the king, 'but only one among them has golden hair. If you find her you may take her with you; but if you make a mistake she will remain with us, and you will have to return empty-handed.'

Georgy felt much embarrassed, not knowing what course to take.

'Buzz, buzz, come walk round these young girls, and I will tell you which is yours.'

Thus spoke the fly whose life Georgy had saved.

Thus reassured he walked boldly round, pointing at them one after the other and saying, 'This one has not the golden hair, nor this one either, nor this. . . .'

Suddenly, having been told by the fly, he cried, 'Here we are: this is Zlato Vlaska, even she herself. I take her for my own, she whom I have won, and for whom I have paid the price with many cares. You will not refuse her me this time.'

'Indeed, you have guessed aright,' replied the king.

The princess rose from her seat, and letting fall her head dress, exposed to full view all the splendour of her wonderful hair, which seemed like a waterfall of golden rays, and covered her from head to foot. The glorious light that shone from it dazzled the young man's eyes, and he immediately fell in love with her.

The king provided his daughter with gifts worthy of a queen, and she left her father's palace in a manner befitting a royal bride. The journey back was accomplished without any mishaps.

On their arrival the old king was delighted at the sight of Zlato Vlaska, and danced with joy. Splendid and costly preparations were made for the wedding. His Majesty then said to Georgy, 'You robbed me of the secret of animal language. For this I intended to have your head cut off and your body thrown to birds of prey. But as you have served me so faithfully and won the princess for my bride I will lessen the punishment – that is, although you will be executed, yet you shall be buried with all the honours worthy of a superior officer.'

So the sentence was carried out, cruelly and unjustly. After the execution the Maid with Hair of Gold begged the king to make her a present of Georgy's body, and the monarch was so much in love that he could not refuse his intended bride anything.

Zlato Vlaska with her own hands replaced the head on the body, and sprinkled it with the Water of Death. Immediately the separated parts became one again. Upon this she poured the Water of Life, and Georgy returned to life, fresh as a young roebuck, his face radiant with health and youth.

'Ah me! How well I have slept,' said he, rubbing his eyes.

'Yes; no one could have slept better,' answered the princess, smiling, 'but without me you would have slept through eternity.'

When the old king saw Georgy restored to life, and looking younger, handsomer and more vigorous than ever, he too wanted to be made young again. He therefore ordered his servants to cut off his head and sprinkle it with the Life-Giving Water. They cut it off, but he did not come to life again, although they sprinkled his body with all the water that was left. Perhaps they made some mistake in using the wrong water, for the head and body were joined, but life itself never returned, there being no water of Life left for that purpose. No one knew where to get any, and none understood the language of animals.

So, to make a long story short, Georgy was proclaimed king, and the Maid with Hair of Gold, who really loved him, became his queen.

The Golden Bird

A long time ago there was a King who had a beautiful pleasure-garden behind his palace and in it stood a tree which grew golden apples. As the apples ripened they were counted but the very next morning one was missing and when this was reported to the King he ordered that watch should be kept under the tree every night.

The King had three sons and at nightfall he sent the eldest to keep watch but by midnight he was overcome by sleep and by morning another apple was missing. The following night the second son had to keep watch but he did no better for by midnight he too was fast asleep and in the morning another apple had gone. It was now the turn of the third son and he was quite ready to go and watch but the king had little confidence in him and thought he would fare no better than his brothers but he finally gave his consent. The young lad lay down under the tree, kept watch and did not let sleep get the better of him. But when the clock struck twelve something rustled in the air and he saw, in the moonlight, a bird flying by whose feathers were of gleaming gold. The bird settled on the tree and had just picked off one of the apples when the youth shot an arrow at it. The bird flew off, however, dropping one of its feathers as it got away. The Prince picked it up and in the morning took it to the King, telling him what had happened. The King then summoned his Council, every one of which declared that a feather like that was worth more than his whole kingdom.

'If that feather is of such great value,' said the King, 'one is not enough; I must and will have the whole bird.'

So the eldest son now set off in search of the bird, thinking he was clever enough to find it without much delay. When he had gone some distance he saw a fox sitting by the edge of a forest. He aimed his gun at it but the fox cried out, 'Don't shoot and I'll give some good advice. You are now on the road to the Golden Bird and this evening you will arrive at a village where you will find two inns standing opposite each other. One will be brightly lit up with much revelry going on inside, but don't go into that one. Go into the other one, though it won't seem much of a place to you.'

How can such a stupid beast give me a reasonable piece of advice? thought the Prince and pulled the trigger but missed and the fox turned tail and fled into the woods. The Prince continued his journey and in the evening came to the village with the two inns. In one singing and dancing were going on but the other looked pretty miserable and abandoned. I'd be a fool, he thought, to go into that wretched-looking haunt when there's this nice one just opposite. So he went into the jolly one and lived there like a lord, forgetting all about the Golden Bird, his father and all the good advice.

When a long time had elapsed and the eldest son showed no sign of coming back home, the second son set out in quest of the Golden Bird. He too met the fox just as his elder brother had and got the same good advice which he likewise ignored, for when he arrived at the two inns and saw his brother standing at the window of one and heard the noise of jollification emerging, he couldn't resist his brother's invitation to join him. So he went in and lived a life of pleasure.

Again time passed and now the King's youngest son wanted to try his luck, but his father refused to let him go. It's no use, he thought, he'll be less likely to find the Golden Bird than his brothers and if any mishap should befall him he won't be able to do anything about it; he lacks the wit. Finally, however, the King gave in and allowed his son to go, for otherwise he gave him no peace. Once more the fox was sitting outside the forest and once more gave his good advice in

return for his life. 'Don't worry, little fox,' said the good-natured Prince, 'I will do you no harm.'

'You won't regret it,' said the fox. 'Get on my tail and you will travel faster.' He had scarcely seated himself than the fox began to run and away they flew over hedge and ditch at such speed that his hair whistled in the wind. When they came to the village the Prince dismounted and, following the fox's advice, and without even turning to look around him, went straight into the wretched-looking inn where he spent a restful night. The next morning when he went out into the fields, he found the fox already there and he said, 'I will tell something else you must do. Go straight on from here and you will ultimately get to a castle in front of which there will be a whole company of soldiers, but you don't have to worry about them for they will all be asleep and snoring. Carry on straight through them and through all the rooms and at last you will come to an apartment where the Golden Bird hangs in a wooden cage. Nearby stands a golden cage, empty, for show, but beware! Do *not* take the bird out of its common cage and place it in the golden one or something nasty will happen.' With those words the fox stretched out his tail and the Prince seated himself on it. Away they flew, over hill and dale, their hair whistling in the wind.

When he arrived at the castle he found everything just as the fox had said – the Golden Bird in a wooden cage and a golden cage near it *and* the three golden apples just lying around on the floor. The Prince thought it would be stupid to leave the beautiful bird in a common, ugly little cage, so he opened the door, caught it and placed it in the golden one. But at that moment the bird let out a piercing shriek, the soldiers woke, rushed in and led him off to prison. The following morning he was summoned before the court and, as he confessed to everything, he was sentenced to death. Nevertheless, said the King, his life would be spared on one condition: that he should bring him the Golden Horse which gallops faster than the wind, and, in addition, he would receive the Golden Bird as a reward.

So the Prince set out, sorrowful and sighing: where *was* he to find that Golden Horse? Then all at once he saw his old friend the fox sitting by the roadside.

'You see what's happened,' said he, 'because you didn't listen to me. Still, be of good courage. I will look after you and tell you how you may find the Golden Horse. Carry straight on along this road till you come to a castle and in the stable there stands the Golden Horse. The stable-lads will be lying sound asleep snoring, so you can quietly lead the horse away. Only there's one thing you must beware of. Put the saddle of wood and leather on his back and *not* the golden one hanging close by or something nasty will happen.' Then the fox stretched out its tail, the Prince seated himself on it and away they flew again over hill and dale, their hair whistling in the wind.

Everything went just as the fox had said. The Prince went into the stable where the Golden Horse stood, but just as he was about to saddle it with the wooden one he thought, 'It would be a shame not to put the golden saddle on such a noble animal, it is really only what is due to him.' But scarcely had it touched the horse's back than it began neighing loudly. The stable-lads woke up, seized the Prince and made him captive. The next morning he was taken before the court and sentenced to death. But the King offered to spare his life and let him have the Golden Horse if he would bring him the beautiful Princess out of the golden castle.

With heavy heart the Prince set out but to his great good fortune he soon met the faithful fox. 'I really ought to leave you to your fate,' he said, 'but I'm sorry for you and once again I'll help you out of your trouble. Your road to the Golden Castle lies straight ahead of you. You will arrive there about evening time and at night when everything is quiet the beautiful Princess will make her way to the bathhouse to take a bath. As she walks along spring up and give her a kiss and she will follow you. Then you can lead her away with you but do not allow her to take leave of her parents first or something nasty will happen.' Then once more the fox stretched out his tail, the Prince seated himself on it and away they flew over hill and dale with the wind whistling in their hair.

When he got to the Castle, things were just as the fox had described. He waited till midnight when everybody was fast asleep and the beautiful young maiden went to take her bath. He sprang forward and kissed her. She was quite willing to go with him but she begged him earnestly, with tears in her eyes, to allow her first to take leave of her parents. At first he resisted her entreaties but as she wept and fell at his feet, he at last gave in. Scarcely had she stepped up to her father's bed when he woke up and so did everyone else in the Castle. The young Prince was seized and taken prisoner.

The following morning the King said to him, 'Your life is forfeit and you can only find mercy if you level down the mountain which blocks the view from my window. This must be done within eight days and if you accomplish this task you shall have my daughter as reward.'

The Prince began his digging and shovelling without rest but when on the seventh day he saw how little progress he had made and all his work had achieved almost nothing at all, he became very downcast indeed and gave up all hope. On the evening of that day, however, the fox appeared and said, 'You don't deserve any help from me but go away and get some sleep and I'll do the work.' When he woke up next morning and looked out of the window the mountain had vanished. Full of joy he hurried to the King and told him his condition had been fulfilled and whether he liked it or not, he must stand by his word and give up his daughter.

So they both set out together and it wasn't long before the faithful fox had caught up with them. 'You have indeed done well,' he said, 'but the Golden Horse must also be awarded to the Maiden of the Golden Castle.'

'But how am I to get it?' asked the Prince.

'I will tell you,' replied the fox. 'First take the beautiful maiden to the King who sent you to the Golden Castle. There will be unheard of joy and they will lead out the Golden Horse to you. Mount it at once, give everyone a handshake and to the Princess last of all. Then hold her firmly, pull her up beside you with a swing and gallop away. No one will catch up with you for the horse goes faster than the wind.'

All this was happily done and the Prince rode away on the Golden Horse with the beautiful maiden. The fox appeared yet again and he said to the Prince, 'Now I will help you to get the Golden Bird. When you are near the Castle where the bird is, let the maid dismount and I will take her into my care. Then ride into the courtyard of the Castle, where the sight of the Golden Horse will bring great rejoicing and they will give you the Golden Bird. As soon as the cage is in your hands, ride back to us and take up the maid again.'

When this had been successfully completed and the Prince was about to ride off with his treasures, the fox said, 'Now you must pay me back for my help.'

'What is it that you require?' asked the Prince.

'When we reach that wood, shoot me dead and cut off my head and paws.'

'What gratitude that would be!' said the Prince. 'I cannot possibly grant you that.'

'Then if you will not do it,' said the fox, 'I must abandon you but before I go I will give you one more piece of good advice. Beware of two things: buy no gallows-flesh and do not sit by the edge of a well.' So saying, he ran off into the wood.

The young Prince thought, What a strange creature! What odd fancies he has! Who would buy gallows-flesh! And I've never had the slightest desire to sit on the edge of a well. He continued his ride with the beautiful maid and the road led him through the village where his two brothers had stopped. There was a great to-do and uproar going on and he asked what it was all about. It appeared that two people were about to be hanged and when he got nearer he saw it was his two brothers; they had committed all kinds of evil deeds and used up all their possessions. He asked whether they could not be set free. 'Yes, if you are willing to pay enough,' was the answer, 'but why waste your money on these wicked men?'

He didn't stop to think, paid up the money and when they were freed they all journeyed off together. They came to the wood where they had first met the fox. It was pleasant and cool there for the sun outside had been very hot and the two brothers said, 'Let us sit down here by the well to eat and drink and rest a little.' Their brother consented and during the conversation he quite forgot the fox's advice and sat down by the edge of the well, not prepared for any foul play. But his two brothers threw him backwards into the well and made off home to their father, taking with them the lovely maid, the horse and the bird.

'We have brought you', they told him, 'not only the Golden Bird but the Golden Horse and the fair maid from the golden castle.' There was great joy at this but the horse would not eat, the bird would not sing and the maid just sat and wept. Their young brother, however, did not perish. Luckily the well was dry and he fell on to some soft moss without any harm. But he could not get out. Even in this trouble the faithful fox did not forsake him. He came leaping down and rebuked him for not following his advice. 'But I can't leave you to your fate. I will help you get back to the light of day.' He told him to take hold of his tail and he dragged him up to the top. 'You are not

[142]

yet out of danger,' said the fox, 'for your brothers, being unsure about your death, have surrounded the wood with spies and they will kill you if they spot you.'

A poor old man was sitting by the wayside and the Prince changed clothes with him and in this disguise he managed to reach the King's court. Nobody recognized him but the bird began to sing, the horse began to eat and the fair maid stopped weeping. In great wonder the King asked, 'What does all this mean?' The maid answered, 'I do not know but before I was sad and now I'm happy. It is as though my true bridegroom had come.' She told him all that had happened although the two brothers had threatened to kill her if she revealed anything. The King ordered every person in the Castle to be brought before him and among them came the Prince dressed as an old man all in rags. But the maid knew him immediately and fell on his neck. The evil brothers were seized and put to death. And the Prince married the beautiful maiden and was made the King's heir.

But what happened to the poor old fox? A long time afterwards the Prince once again went out into the woods where the fox met him and said, 'Now you have everything you could wish for but to my ill-luck there is no end. It lies within your powers to release me.' And he again begged the Prince to shoot him dead and cut off his head and paws.

The Prince yielded to his earnest request and no sooner was it done than the fox changed into a man who turned out to be none other than the beautiful Princess's brother – freed at last from the spell that lay upon him. And so now nothing was lacking in their happiness for the rest of their lives.

The Golden Candelabra

There was a time and there wasn't a time in the long ago when a rich merchant lived in the city of Nishapoor. He was a widower and lived alone, except for his daughter whose name was Pari. The merchant loved her more than anything in the world, and for this reason he kept her locked in his house in a velvet-lined room so that no harm could befall her.

Pari grew tall and graceful. Her hair was as black as a blackbird's wing and her eyes were like two sapphires. Her father gave her everything her heart desired – silken gowns and ivory chairs and a bed of ebony wood. When the weather was warm, she fanned herself with a fan of peacock feathers.

One day, Pari said to her father, 'Father, you have granted me every wish. Now that I am sixteen, I wish to go into the city like other people and see the world.'

'My child,' said the merchant, 'this wish shall also be granted. You are soon to be married to Golhak Khan, the tea merchant. I have arranged it for you. Then you will ride to his fine house in a carriage and you will see the world in all its ugliness and all its beauty.'

Golhak Khan was an old man with a red beard. He was a kind

man, but Pari did not want to be married to him. That night she lay upon her bed of ebony and wept.

The next day, she said to her father, 'Father, you have granted me every wish. It is dark in my chamber. I wish for a golden candelabra that holds a hundred candles, so my chamber will be as bright as the great world outside.'

'You shall have your wish, my child,' said her father, and he sent out messengers to find the finest goldsmith in Persia.

The goldsmith came from Isfahan, and, when Pari was alone with him, she said, 'If you make my golden candelabra exactly as I tell you, I shall give you my fan of peacock feathers and an ivory chair for your wife to sit in when she spins.'

'Speak, my lady, I shall obey,' said the goldsmith.

'And you must promise on the head of your wife that you will never tell my father the secret of the golden candelabra,' said Pari.

And, being a greedy fellow, he did not want to refuse the extra gifts. 'My lips are sealed,' he said. 'And besides, I shall be far away in Isfahan.'

So, Pari told him to fashion the candelabra in the shape of a date-palm tree with one hundred branches of beaten gold. Each branch held a candle that would burn for a week. And, in the trunk of the golden palm tree, the goldsmith made a secret door – as Pari told him to – so finely fitted that no one could tell it was there.

When the candelabra was finished, the goldsmith returned to Isfahan, and the candelabra was placed in Pari's chamber. One night, when her father was asleep, she took seven loaves of bread and a jug of goat's milk and went to the candelabra. She pressed the hidden jewel which opened the secret door, and she stepped inside the golden trunk. Then she closed the door after her.

The next morning, when her father came to greet her, he found her room empty. He was beside himself with grief. He sent messengers through the city offering rewards to anyone who could give him news of his beloved daughter. But Pari was nowhere to be found. After five days, the merchant went to a wise man. 'My daughter has vanished,' he said. 'What can I do to recover her?'

The wise man answered. 'The golden candelabra has brought misfortune to your house. Sell it, and your daughter will return to you.'

So the merchant shipped the golden candelabra to Samarkand, where it was placed in a shop window for sale. The very next day, the

Prince of Samarkand came riding by on his horse as he returned from hunting. When he saw the golden candelabra, he reined in his horse, and entered the shop himself and bought it. The candelabra was placed in the Prince's chamber near a window where he could see its glistening branches in the dawn light as he woke up.

Pari, who had been inside the trunk of the golden candelabra all this time, had finished her seven loaves of bread and had drunk her jug of goat's milk, and she was hungry. 'I must open the secret door and find something to eat or I shall never see the great world,' she said to herself. 'I wonder where I am.' She put her ear to the secret door and listened.

She heard voices, for the Prince was talking with his servant. So, Pari kept very still and waited, growing hungrier and hungrier. At last, the Prince, who was tired from his long day's hunting, fell asleep without eating his supper. The room was silent, and Pari noiselessly opened the secret door and stepped out.

She found herself in a chamber hung with rich damask and tiled with black marble. How beautiful the world is, she thought, as she looked around in delight.

She did not see the Prince, who was fast asleep inside the curtains of his bed, but she saw the Prince's supper laid out on a small table. She tiptoed across the room and ate up all his food. Then she returned to the golden candelabra, stepped inside, closed the secret door after her, and fell asleep.

Next morning, when the Prince awoke, he remembered that he had forgotten to eat his supper. He rose and went across the room to the table where his supper had been. Every plate was empty.

He called his servant. 'Did anyone enter my room in the night when I was asleep?' he asked.

'No, master,' said the servant. 'I have been on guard outside the door all night.'

The next night, the Prince again fell asleep after hunting without eating, and again Pari crept from the candelabra and ate his supper. This happened for three nights. On the fourth night, the Prince decided to stay awake. He went to bed as usual, but he left the curtains of his bed partly open. At midnight, he heard a soft noise like the rustle of silk.

Suddenly, the trunk of the candelabra opened and Pari stepped out. She went across the room, sat down at the little table and began peeling an apple. The Prince thought she was the most beautiful creature he had ever seen, and his heart was heavy.

His father, the King, had already affianced him to the Princess of Turan, who would arrive in Samarkand within a month for the marriage. The Princess of Turan was bad-tempered, but she was the richest princess in the East, and his marriage to her would bring wealth and prosperity to Samarkand.

For many nights the Prince remained awake until midnight, and each night Pari came out and ate his supper. He began to order rare delicacies from the palace kitchen – thrushes' tongues and turtle eggs from the sands of the Nile, all seasoned with spices from the Spice Islands. He grew angry when such rarities could not be found instantly. All through the palace people began to say, 'How difficult the Prince has become. He has fallen in love with his stomach.'

Then, one night, the Prince placed his ring beside his supper plate. At midnight, Pari crept as usual from the trunk of the golden candelabra and went to the table. The Prince stepped out from behind the curtains.

'Have no fear,' he said. 'No harm shall come to you.'

His face was so kind and his voice so gentle that Pari was not frightened. The Prince came and sat beside her at the table and they ate the supper together side by side, while Pari told him her story. When she had finished, the Prince said, 'I have loved you since the first night I saw you, but, alas, I am to marry the bad-tempered Princess of Turan. The wedding feast will be celebrated next week.'

Pari wept and said, 'It was my wish to see the great world. But now I wish to see no more. I shall return to my father in Nishapoor.'

'Do not desert me,' cried the Prince, pressing her hands. He placed his ring upon her finger and said, 'With this ring I shall wed thee. Do not doubt me and all will be well.'

So, Pari returned at dawn to her hiding place within the golden trunk. Next day, the Prince said to his father, the King, 'Sire, I do not wish to marry the Princess of Turan. She is bad-tempered and has an evil heart.'

But the King said, 'She has done nothing wrong to you, my son. It is true that people say she is bad-tempered, but wait. Soon the Princess will arrive from Turan. Then you will see that she is as beautiful as a star.'

For another week, Pari lived inside the golden candelabra during the day and at night she shared the Prince's supper with him. They talked and laughed and were happy, and did not think of tomorrow.

But the day arrived, at last, when the gorgeous caravan of the Princess of Turan entered the gates of Samarkand. A parade passed out through the gates in her honour and the Grand Vizier rode on a black horse to welcome her. She was given a suite of rooms in the palace, and the King himself invited her to a midnight feast.

But the Prince was absent from the feast, for he was in his chamber eating apples with Pari.

The Princess of Turan, who was very beautiful but whose heart was evil, said to the King, 'Where is my betrothed?'

The King said, 'You will meet him in good time, my lady.'

The Princess of Turan was angry, but she hid her bad temper. She excused herself early from the feast and went to her rooms. There she called her slave-girl. 'Go through all the palace,' she commanded. 'Find where the Prince is and why he failed to receive me.'

The slave-girl walked through the hallways of the palace, listening and watching. When she came to the Prince's door, she asked the guard, 'Where is your master, the Prince?'

'He is inside this room taking supper with his beloved,' the guard answered.

'Who is his beloved?'

'No one knows. By day she vanishes, by night she appears.'

The slave-girl returned to her mistress and told her what she had learned. Then the Princess of Turan ordered the slave-girl to change clothes with her. Dressed as a slave, with her face veiled, the Princess of Turan went to the Prince's door. The guard was fast asleep on the floor, so the Princess peeped through the keyhole. She saw the Prince and Pari laughing together. Fire and rage consumed her heart and she waited there until dawn came. She saw Pari disappear within the trunk of the golden candelabra and she saw the Prince retire to his bed.

When she was sure the Prince was asleep, the Princess of Turan softly opened the door of his chamber and entered. Taking a torch from the fireside, she carefully lighted the one hundred candles of the golden candelabra. Soon the room was blazing with light. The heat from the hundred candles began to warm the golden trunk of the candelabra. Soon it was as hot as fire.

Pari, who was asleep inside, woke with a terrible feeling of being

[148]

roasted. She could not breathe. She thrust open the door and fell on to the floor in a faint.

The Princess of Turan ran to the guard, shook him awake, and whispered, 'An evil fairy has bewitched this room. I have saved your master, the Prince, from her evil magic. Come quickly and take her away, but do not wake your master.'

The guard ran into the room, wrapped Pari in a rug and, thinking she was dead, threw her into the river which flowed past the castle wall.

The cold water revived Pari and she began to struggle. The swift-flowing water carried her downstream, where an old fisherman sat on the river bank netting fish. He saw her, threw out his net, and dragged her to shore. Then he carried her to his hut, put her on his straw pallet, and fed her on warm sheep's milk.

When Pari opened her eyes, the old fisherman said, 'Pretty maiden, where is your home?'

Pari answered, 'My home is in the golden candelabra.'

The fisherman said, 'Where is the golden candelabra?'

'Alas,' said Pari, 'I do not know.'

So the fisherman said, 'I am without wife to warm me or child to help me in my labours. You shall stay with me and be my daughter until you find your home again in the golden candelabra.'

So Pari remained with the fisherman in his little hut. She cooked for him and sewed for him and helped him mend his nets. One day, the fisherman came home from the river and said, 'My daughter, the town crier is calling through Samarkand. Our beloved Prince is sick. He refuses to eat. The most expensive meals are prepared for him, but he will not eat them, though only a short while ago he was supping on thrushes' tongues and turtle eggs from the sands of the Nile. He is growing thin and sickly and this is not right, for he is to be married to the Princess of Turan.'

Pari said nothing, but her heart was sore, for now she knew that her golden candelabra had been in the chamber of the Prince of Samarkand, and that he was lost to her for ever.

The fisherman went on. 'The town crier has asked that every cook throughout the countryside prepare a dish to tempt the Prince's appetite. All the women are taking food to the palace and each dish is set before the Prince. Let us hope that something tempts him to eat and get well again.'

[149]

Pari said, 'I, too, shall prepare a dish for the Prince. I shall prepare a bowl of brown broth.'

The fisherman was dismayed, for he thought that peasant broth in an earthen bowl would not be accepted by the Prince. But, as he loved Pari, he agreed to take her broth to the palace. Pari cooked some lamb bones with yellow peas and onions and garlic until the broth was rich and brown. Then she poured it into a covered bowl so it wouldn't get cold. When the old fisherman was not looking, she took the Prince's ring from her finger and dropped it into the broth. Then she gave the bowl to the fisherman.

He carried it to the palace, where the guard halted him. 'I have brought a dish to tempt the Prince,' the fisherman said.

'What do you have?' asked the guard and he lifted the cover of the earthen bowl. 'Ugh!' he said. 'Peasant's brown broth! Do you think our Prince, who can't bear to eat thrushes' tongues, will be tempted by your crude brown broth?'

'It is from the hands of a girl nobody knows. She came to me from a golden candelabra,' the fisherman said, so the guard let him pass.

The fisherman walked up the carriageway and through the great marble arch into the palace. At last, he was led to the Prince's chamber. There sat the Prince, pale and wan. Around him on a dozen tables were silver salvers bearing spicy, steaming dishes – plates of lobster tails and peahens roasted in pomegranate juice and fish from the north sea simmered in ass's milk. But the Prince sat staring at the golden candelabra and eating nothing.

'Great Prince,' said the fisherman, 'may I offer a bowl of brown broth made by the hands of a maiden?'

The Prince looked at him and listened to his humble words. He took the earthen bowl of brown broth and lifted the cover. The broth smelled so good that he dipped in his spoon. He smiled as he tasted the broth and he began to eat.

At the bottom of the bowl, he discovered his own ring. 'Old man,' he cried, 'who has prepared this broth?'

'My daughter has prepared it,' the fisherman said. He was frightened and hung his head.

The Prince commanded in a stern voice, 'Bring your daughter before me at once.'

The old fisherman hurried away, half dead with fear. He ran home and said to Pari, 'My daughter, you must run away, you must leave

[151]

this town at once. The Prince ate your broth and as he came to the last bite, he grew angry. His eyes flashed fire.'

'Where shall I go?' asked Pari.

The old fisherman said, 'You must follow your destiny. I shall roll you again into the rug and throw you again into the river. I broke the thread of your destiny when I took you out of the river, and now we shall both be punished.'

The old fisherman ran to get the rug, but just then there was a hammering on the door of the hut. The Prince's guards entered and took out their swords and barred the door. Then they marched Pari and the old fisherman to the palace. Pari was trembling with fear, for she did not know why the Prince had been angry when he found her ring at the bottom of the broth. He has forgotten me, she told herself.

When the fisherman and Pari were led into the Prince's chamber, the fisherman threw himself on the floor and begged for mercy. But the Prince had already jumped up from his throne. He ran across the room and knelt at Pari's feet. Everyone was astonished to see the Prince of Samarkand on his knees before a humble fishermaiden.

Then the Prince rose and led Pari to a chair. He said to the old fisherman, 'Forgive me, ancient fisherman. I thought you had stolen the ring which I found in the broth. Rise, and you shall be rewarded, for you have brought me my beloved.'

So Pari and the Prince found each other again, and when Pari told her story to the King, the Princess of Turan was sent back home in disgrace.

Pari married the Prince and invited her own father from Nishapoor to the wedding. At the wedding feast, every guest had a bowl of brown broth made by Pari herself. And the Golden Candelabra always stood in their chamber and brought them good fortune for the rest of their lives.

The Golden Knucklebone

Once upon a time there lived, in a camp on a great plain, a man and his wife and their young son, whose name was Altin. This boy, Altin, possessed a golden knucklebone, and when he played at knucklebones with his comrades, he always won.

Well now, Altin's father kept a great many horses, which he pastured on the plain; and it was by buying and selling these horses that he earned his living. So one day Altin's father drove his horses down to a pool to drink. In this pool there lived a Water Cat, and as the horses bent their heads to drink, the Water Cat put a magic spell on them. And there they were, whisking their tails, stamping their feet, trembling all over, but not able to lift their heads from the water.

'Let go my herd, you wretched creature!' shouted Altin's father.

'Why should I?' said the Water Cat.

'Because they're mine, not yours!' shouted Altin's father.

'Well then,' said the Water Cat, 'if you will promise to give me Altin's golden knucklebone, I will set your horses free.'

So Altin's father promised. He said, 'Tomorrow I am going to move camp. I will leave the knucklebone buried in the ashes outside our present camp, and you can fetch it.'

Then the Water Cat let the horses go; and after they had drunk their fill, Altin's father drove them home.

That evening he said to his wife, 'You had better get busy packing up. Tomorrow we are moving camp. I must go to a place where there is better grazing for the horses.'

So the wife packed up, and then they went to their beds. Before he got into bed, Altin had laid his golden knucklebone on the floor beside him. And when he slept, his father came and took the knucklebone, and buried it in the ashes of their camp fire.

Next morning all was bustle. And what with helping his father to round up the horses, and loading the tent on to the back of one, and all their goods and chattels on to the backs of others, Altin never gave a thought to his knucklebone.

Well, they travelled for many hours, and came to a pleasant grassy place near a briskly flowing stream that was bordered by trees. There they pitched their tent and unpacked their goods; and it was then that Altin realized that his golden knucklebone was missing.

'Where is it, where is my knucklebone?' he asked his mother. 'Did you pack it in one of the pots and pans?'

'No,' said his mother. 'Your father left it in the old camping site. He buried it in the ashes of the fire.'

Altin went to his father. 'I am going to ride back to our old camp, to fetch my golden knucklebone,' he said.

'That will be a waste of time,' said his father.

'I am going,' said Altin again. 'Which horse shall I take?'

His father said, 'Shake a bridle.'

Altin shook a bridle: and a poor little colt, very shaky on its legs, came ambling up to him.

'Father,' said Altin, 'I cannot ride that colt. What shall I do?'

'Shake the bridle, shake the bridle,' answered his father. 'Isn't that what I told you?'

So Altin shook the bridle again. But not one of the herd of horses so much as turned a head. Only the poor little colt came to stand close at his side, and rubbed its thin little nose against Altin's sleeve.

'Saddle and bridle the colt,' said Altin's father.

So Altin, not very willingly, did that. What happened? The colt turned into a magnificent chestnut Arab stallion. And Altin vaulted into the saddle, shouted 'Hurrah!' and galloped off.

That stallion went so fast that it overtook the wind that blew before it; and the wind that fell behind it could never catch up with it again. In a very short time Altin was back at the old camping site. What did he see there? He saw the Water Cat sitting in the ashes of the camp fire, playing with the golden knucklebone.

'Hey, Water Cat, that's *my* knucklebone! Hand it up here to me!'

'No, Altin, no, I can't stand up. I've got a bad back. You get off your horse, and take it out of my paw.'

(That Water Cat was cunning, and he had magic powers. Once he got hold of Altin, he meant to turn him into a frog.)

But before Altin had time to dismount, the chestnut stallion lowered his head, snatched the golden knucklebone out of the Water Cat's paws and galloped off.

The Water Cat screamed, the Water Cat jumped up: he clapped his paws together. And there stood a big dun-coloured horse. The Water Cat leaped on to the dun-coloured horse's back, and galloped after Altin.

Altin's chestnut stallion was galloping, galloping.

The Water Cat's dun-coloured horse was galloping, galloping.

And the Water Cat's horse cried out:

> *My legs won't go at such a rate,*
> *Chestnut brother, kindly wait.*

Then Altin's stallion turned his head over his shoulder and called back:

> *Your legs may run until they drop,*
> *Dun-coloured brother, I won't stop.*

So on he galloped, and on and on, and came to a stream with trees growing on the bank. (It was the same stream that farther on flowed past the wide grassy place where Altin's father had now pitched his tent.) But the stallion was drawing his breath in great gasps, and he panted out, 'Altin, I can go no farther. You climb up into a tree, and I will change myself into a fox.'

So Altin jumped off the stallion's back, and climbed up into a tree; and the stallion turned into a fox and ran away to hide under some bushes.

Then along came the Water Cat on the dun-coloured horse, galloping, galloping. He looked up into the tree, he saw Altin, he screamed, he jumped down from his horse, he clapped his paws together, he changed the horse into an axe, and began to chop down the tree.

And as he was chopping, he was singing:

> Master Altin Up-a-tree,
> Don't you think to hide from me.
> If you'd call your life your own,
> Throw me down the knucklebone!

But Altin called down out of the tree, 'It is my knucklebone, *mine*! You shall not have it!'

So the Water Cat went on chopping. He had chopped nearly half through the tree trunk when the Fox (that was the stallion) came out from under the bushes.

'Eh, little grandfather Water Cat,' said the Fox. 'You'll wear yourself to a shadow chopping away like that! Here, let me have a go!'

'No, no, *no*!' screamed the Water Cat. 'I can manage! I can manage!'

'Manage!' laughed Fox. 'You'll be managing to drop down dead, very soon! Come on now, give me the axe!'

'Well,' said the Water Cat, 'perhaps I should be the better for a little snooze.' And he handed the axe to Fox and lay down among some ferns. Next moment he was snoring. So then Fox threw the axe far out into the stream, he breathed on the tree and made it whole again and ran off to hide under the bushes.

Water Cat was having a pleasant dream. He was dreaming that the tree had fallen, and Altin with it, and that he was crunching up Altin's bones. But when he woke, the tree was standing quite undamaged, and Altin was still safe up in its branches. And Water Cat couldn't find his axe. However, by clapping his paws and stamping and screaming he at last got another axe (yes, an axe came from somewhere or other and dropped into Water Cat's paw.) So he began to chop at the tree again.

Chop, chop, chop! It was hard work. Water Cat didn't like hard work. He was screaming at the tree, telling it to fall. But the tree said, 'I shan't fall until you've chopped right through my trunk – why should I?'

So Water Cat had to go on chopping.

Meanwhile the Fox (who as you will remember was the stallion in disguise) came out from under the bush where he had been hiding. When he went in under the bush he had a russet coat, but now he had a black one. (He had changed his colour by changing his thoughts from red to black.)

So now he went to the Water Cat and said: 'Eh, little grandaddy, whatever are you doing? You ought to know better than to go working away like that at your age! Come, I am young and strong; if you want to cut down the tree, give me the axe, I'll have the tree down in no time!'

'No, no, *No!*' shrieked the Water Cat. 'I've been fooled by one Fox – and shall I be fooled by another?'

'Ah,' said the Fox, 'that must have been the russet-coloured fellow. He has been a scatter-brained deceiver from his youth up. But *I* am not scatter-brained. I am serious. My thoughts are as my coat: solemn, unspotted. Come, give me the axe.'

Well, if that Water Cat wasn't a stupid-head! He handed Fox the axe and lay down to sleep again. Soon he was snoring. So then Fox threw the axe into the river. He breathed on the tree and made it whole again. Then he went once more to hide under the bushes.

By and by Water Cat woke up. He looked round for the Fox, he looked round for his axe, both had gone. And there was the tree standing quite undamaged. He was screaming with rage. But by scraping his feet and clapping his paws, he got another axe, and began to chop at the tree again. He chopped and he chopped and he chopped.

The tree was moaning: 'It hurts, it hurts! I shan't be able to stay up much longer.' So the Fox (the stallion in disguise) came out from under the bushes, turned a somersault, and changed his coat from black to white. He went to the Water Cat and said, 'Old fellow, let me have a go! I'm a dab at chopping – give me the axe!'

But the Water Cat screamed out: 'I've been deceived twice! I'm not listening to foxes any more. Get away – get away!'

Chop, chop, chop: The tree was groaning, the tree was swaying. The Fox (the stallion in disguise) looked up into the branches. 'Oh Altin, what shall we do?' But a Sparrow that was perched in the tree chirruped, 'Altin's father has two big dogs. Shall I go and call them?'

'Yes, yes, my Sparrow, fly swiftly, my Sparrow!'

So the Sparrow flew off as fast as ever he could, and came to the camp of Altin's father. The two big dogs, Akkulak and Sakkulak, were tied up outside the camp. But when they got the Sparrow's message, they bit through the thongs that held them, and rushed off along the way to the tree. The Water Cat heard their panting breath. He looked round and saw the cloud of dust the dogs were raising.

'Boy, boy,' he called to Altin, 'what is that I see coming along the road?'

And Altin answered, 'I am not sure, Water Cat. Either it is grief for you and joy for me. Or it is joy for you and grief for me.'

'Grief, grief, grief for me!' shrieked the Water Cat, as the big dogs came racing up.

And he flung down his axe and jumped into the river.

Wrow, wrow, wrow! growling and snarling those two big dogs, Akkulak and Sakkulak, jumped into the river after the Water Cat. Altin slid down from the tree, the White Fox changed himself back into the stallion, and the stallion and Altin hurried to the river bank.

'Altin,' said the stallion, 'there will be a fight under the water. If the dogs kill the Water Cat we shall see black bubbles rising. If the Water Cat kills the dogs we shall see red bubbles.'

So they looked and listened. The river water was all in commotion, and they could hear screams, and growls, and fierce barking . . . And then, oh then, a few red bubbles rose. Altin wept, but the stallion said, 'Nay, Altin, maybe the dogs are only wounded. Have a little patience . . . And see, see!' he cried, 'the black bubbles, the black bubbles!'

Yes, in tens, in hundreds, and in thousands, black bubbles were rising and floating away on the surface of the water. And when all the bubbles had disappeared, the two faithful dogs, Akkulak and Sakkulak, came up from the bottom of the river. Akkulak had lost a piece of one ear, Sakkulak had a bleeding paw, but they were jumping round Altin, wagging their tails and panting with joy.

'And now it's time we all went home,' said the stallion. 'But first we must mend that poor tree.' Then the stallion went to the tree and breathed on it. And there it was standing up straight and proud without a single cut in it.

So Altin got on to the stallion's back, and rode to his father's camp, followed by the two dogs, Akkulak and Sakkulak. By the time they reached the camp the sun was setting, and Altin, having lifted the saddle and bridle from the stallion, left him to graze, and went in to get his supper, for he was very hungry.

His father was grumpy, he didn't say anything to Altin. And his mother was still busy unpacking their goods and chattles. It seemed

to Altin a very flat ending to his day's adventure. So, after supper, he went out to say goodnight to the stallion.

'Altin,' said the stallion, 'I am looking into the future.'

'And what do you see in the future, my stallion?'

'I see you grown into a mighty hero, Altin, a hero of many names. I see you fighting and slaying fiery dragons, rescuing captive princesses, overcoming huge giants, and sharp-toothed monsters with many heads. I see you flying on the backs of eagles, battling with sea-serpents, wrecked on the high seas, imprisoned in underground vaults, slain a hundred times, yet a hundred times restored to life. And in every one of these adventures I see myself as your comrade, carrying you into danger, carrying you out of danger again ... But all this is in your future. Now you are just a tired boy. And so, Altin, you had better go to bed.'

The Nightingale and The Speck of Gold

They say that once upon a time, soon after the beginning of the world, all the birds were much the same to look at, except for their different sizes. They were all just sort of brown on top and greyish-white or stone colour underneath, and they all had the same kind of beaks; ordinary, short, straight ones.

Well, one day God was walking round the world, looking at all the wonderful things he'd made, and suddenly it occurred to him that the birds were rather dull and that he could improve them and make them something special. So he told Gabriel to get everything ready and then summon all the birds to assemble on a particular day, because he was going to make them look different and really splendid.

When the day came, there were crowds of birds gathered – all the birds in the world. The meeting-place was a big, green hill, and Gabriel had quite a job getting them all to keep quiet while he counted them and ticked them off on his list to make sure none was missing. And then the magpie stole the list for a joke and when Gabriel got it back again it was a bit scratched and muddy. Anyway, finally he decided that everyone must have arrived (he'd made a mistake, as you'll see) and he told God they were ready to start.

God arrived with a huge bag, full of different beaks, and carrying his paint-box. The colours in the box were self-perpetuating and everlasting, and they were so wonderful and extraordinary that even God wouldn't be able to make any more. He asked the jay politely to be quiet and then explained to all the birds that he'd decided it would be a marvellous idea to paint them, and that each of them would be allowed to choose his own colours and his own beak. The birds cheered and got very excited and then they all sat down or flew about, waiting for their turns and talking to each other about the different colours they were going to have.

The first bird to come up was the macaw and he fairly did himself proud. No one's ever seen anything like it from that day to this. God and Gabriel were careful not to laugh, but they couldn't help just catching each other's eyes as the macaw kept on asking for a bit more of the red and then a bit more of that very bright blue in the corner. When they'd finished, he chose a big, strong, hooked beak that he could crack nuts with, and back he flew to Africa, as pleased as Punch and fairly squawking with pride.

The blackbird came up next, although he hadn't got that name yet. He'd been watching while they painted the macaw and he'd seen the other birds laughing behind their wings. So he chose a beautiful, plain, glossy black, and then he cocked his tail and looked all round and went 'T'ck, t'ck, t'ck,' as much as to say 'Now then, who's going to laugh at that?' All the same, he couldn't resist a bright-yellow beak he saw in the bag, and everyone said it set off the black very well. Before he left he flew up into a beech tree and sang a beautiful song of thanks.

One by one, all the birds came up in their turns and chose their colours. The thrush sat up very straight and still while his breast was dotted with brown spots, and you can just imagine what a lot of trouble the peacock gave before he was satisfied. He couldn't even sing about it either, but God didn't mind. He just went on painting, for he loved all his birds – whinchats and blackcaps, yellow wagtails, waxwings and red-throated swallows. There was one enormous beak that God thought he'd made wrong and he was going to throw it away, but the pelican said, 'Just a moment, Lord, I believe it would suit me very well:' and so it did, for he's kept it ever since.

It was a beautiful summer day and even the humming-birds didn't feel cold. At last, as evening was falling, God saw that there were only a few birds remaining, and he told then that they could go ahead and use up all the paint he had left, because he'd mixed it that morning specially and it wouldn't keep. So the kingfisher and the bee-eater and the green woodpecker and the hoopoe and the oriole and one or two more took him at his word, and had themselves fairly covered with marvellous blues and greens and pinks and yellows.

At last every single bird had come and gone, and there were no beaks left and all the wonderful paint was gone too; and God washed his hands in the brook – What? Well, I don't see why not. It says 'sitteth at the right hand of God' doesn't it? – and he and Gabriel went strolling away down the hill together, feeling pretty tired, I dare say, but very much pleased with their long day's work.

'That's improved the world no end, Lord,' said Gabriel, as they came to the wood at the foot of the hill. 'Just look at that chaffinch sitting on the elder there, with his slate-blue top-knot.'

The chaffinch sang, 'Will you, will you, will you, will you *kiss* me, dear?' and God laughed as he flew away in the twilight, flashing the white feathers along his wings.

Just at that moment they both heard a fluttering and a kind of commotion down in the wood. Something was coming along through the bushes, and evidently in a great hurry too, for the leaves were rustling and twigs were snapping, and yet there was nothing to be seen. They both waited to find out what it could be, but it was nearly dark now and they couldn't make out very much at all.

God was just turning away, when suddenly a little grey-and-brown bird flew out of the hawthorn, piping 'Lord! Lord!' It was the night-ingale. God stretched out his arms and the nightingale perched on his wrist.

'They told me – told me – the blackbird told me just now that you'd asked – you'd asked everybody to come and be painted,' gasped the nightingale. 'He said I ought to have heard about it before, but I live in the thick bushes down in the wood and nobody remembered to come and tell me. I hurried here as soon as I heard. I'm not too late, Lord, am I?'

God looked into the wonderful paint-box. It was absolutely bare. Every single colour was gone, all used up. The little bird looked too, and when he saw the box was empty he couldn't control a sob of bitter disappointment. He felt it was all his own fault, and he was just going to fly away when God noticed the brushes, lying in their place

[163]

at one side of the box. On the tip of one of them was left a glittering speck of gold.

'Just sit here on my finger a moment,' said God, 'and open your beak.'

The little brown bird did as he was told, and God took the brush and gently touched his tongue with the speck of gold. It tasted sharp and burning and he flew away quickly into the bushes. Then, suddenly, he began to sing. No one in all the world had ever heard any bird sing like that. The farmer, driving his cows home to milking, stopped in amazement. The shepherd on the hill forgot his sheep and stood staring into the dusk, and his wife, who was tucking their little boy up in bed, came to the window and listened as though an angel were singing.

God and Gabriel listened too, for a long time, and then they went home. They didn't need to ask the nightingale whether he was happy. It was a quiet night and they could still hear him half a mile away.

The Golden Lads

There once lived a poor man and his wife who had nothing at all except a little hut and they managed to live on the fish they caught, but only just. But one day as the man sat by the water he threw in his net and when he drew it out he found in it a fish that was all gold. And as he gazed at the fish full of wonder, it began to talk and said, 'Listen, good fisher, if you throw me back into the water I'll turn your little hut into a fine castle.'

But the fisherman replied, 'What use will a castle be to me if I've got nothing to eat?'

'Oh, that will be taken care of,' replied the gold fish. 'There'll be a cupboard in the castle and when you open it, you'll find dishes in it full of the most delicious food – as much as you would want.'

'In that case,' said the fisherman, 'I'll do as you wish.'

'Good,' replied the fish, 'but there's one condition: you must not tell a single soul in the whole world how you came by this good fortune; just one little word and it will all disappear.'

The man threw the fish back into the water and went home, but on the spot where his hut used to be stood a great castle. He could scarcely believe his eyes and when he went inside he found his wife smartly dressed in the most beautiful clothes and seated in a splendid room. She looked highly delighted.

'Tell me, husband,' she said, 'how has all this happened? Isn't it marvellous?'

'Yes,' replied her husband, 'I think it's wonderful too, but I'm awfully hungry, so first give me something to eat.'

'But I haven't got anything,' said his wife, 'and in this new house I've no idea where to find anything.'

'No need to worry about that,' said her husband. 'There's a big cupboard over there, just go and open it.'

When the cupboard was opened they found cakes, meat, fruit and wine and the wife laughed with joy. 'Dear husband,' she cried with delight, 'what else could one wish for,' and they sat down and ate and drank.

When they had eaten their fill (and perhaps more), the wife asked, 'Now, husband, tell me where all this wealth comes from.'

'Ah!' he replied, 'don't ask me anything about that. I daren't tell you. If I were to let out the secret to anyone at all, our good luck would disappear.'

'Very well,' she replied, 'if I'm not supposed to know it would be unwise of me to press you.'

But she really wasn't in earnest for she had no peace, day or night, and she teased and pestered her husband so long that he finally lost patience and let out that it all came from a wonderful golden fish which he had caught and then set free again. And no sooner were the words out of his mouth than the fine castle and cupboard disappeared and once again they found themselves sitting in their poor old fishing hut. So now the man had to go back to his old trade again but luck smiled on him and once again he pulled out the gold fish.

'Now listen to me,' said the fish, 'if you throw me back into the water again, I'll give you back the castle and the cupboard full of the best meats. But take good care and do not on any account betray the secret of where they came from because you'll only lose them again.'

'I'll take very good care,' replied the fisherman and threw the fish back into the water. Back at his home he found everything restored to its former splendour, with his wife overjoyed at their good fortune. But her curiosity would give her no peace so that after a few days she began nagging her husband again with questions about how it had all happened and how it all began. The man kept silent for some time but at length she got him so exasperated that he blurted out the secret and so, with his promise broken, the castle disappeared once more and they were again sitting in their little hut.

'There,' said the man, 'you've had your way and we're on the breadline again.'

'Ah,' said his wife, 'I'd rather have it this way, I'd prefer not to have all that wealth if I didn't know where it came from. I wouldn't get a moment's peace.'

The man went back to his fishing and after a little while the same thing happened again, he hauled out the golden fish for the *third* time.

'Listen,' said the fish, 'I can see that I'm destined to keep on falling into your hands. Take me home and cut me into six pieces. Give two pieces to your wife, two to your horse and the remaining two put into the ground and you will get a blessing.'

So the man carried the fish home with him and did what the fish had told him. And then what happened was that two golden lilies grew from the two portions he had put into the ground, his horse had two golden foals and his wife gave birth to twin boys and they too were golden.

Both boys grew up tall and handsome and the foals and lilies grew with them. One day the children said to their father, 'Father, we want to mount on our golden steeds and ride out into the world.' But sorrowfully their father answered, 'How will I manage when you ride away and I won't know how you are faring?'

The boys replied, 'The two golden lilies are here and you will be able to tell from them how things are with us. If they remain fresh, we are well, and if they wilt then we're sick. And if they fall then we're dead.'

So they rode away and came to an inn where there were many people who, as soon as they set eyes on the two golden children, began to jeer and laugh at them. When one of them heard their mocking laughter he felt ashamed; he refused to go any further, turned back and returned home to his father.

But his brother rode on till he came to a large forest. But as he ventured into it, people said to him, 'Better not go there for the forest is full of robbers who will do you no good and, of course, when they see that both you and your horse are golden they will kill you.' But he wasn't going to be scared, saying, 'I must and will ride further.' So he got hold of some bears' skins and covered himself and his horse with them so that no gold at all was visible and rode confidently on into the forest.

When he had ridden some little way he heard a rustling among the bushes and voices talking to one another. On one side someone was saying, 'Here comes one,' and on the other side of him there was a whisper, 'Let him be, he's only a bear-skin hunter and as poor and bald as a church-mouse. What could we do with him?' So the golden lad rode through the forest and came to no harm.

One day he came to a village where he saw a girl who he thought was so beautiful that there couldn't be anyone lovelier in the whole world. And as he felt so great a love for her he went up to her and said, 'I love you with all my heart. Will you be my wife?' And he too found such favour in the girl's eyes that she consented and replied, 'Yes, I will be your wife and be true to you all my life.'

So they were married and right in the midst of their great rejoicing the bride's father came home and when he saw that his daughter was celebrating her wedding he asked in great wonder, 'Where is the bridegroom?' They pointed out to him the golden child who was still wrapped in his bear's skin. The father exclaimed in great anger, 'Never shall a bear-hunter marry my daughter!' And he would have murdered him. But the bride pleaded with all her heart. 'He is, after all, my husband and I love him with all my heart.' And she begged so piteously that her father finally yielded and spared him.

But he still could not get it out of his mind so the next morning he got up early with a wish to see his daughter's husband – was he a common ragged beggar or no? But when he looked into their room who should he see in the bed but a magnificent golden man and the cast-off bear's skin on the ground close by. So he went away thinking to himself, 'What a good thing it was that I controlled my rage or I would have committed a most awful deed.'

Meanwhile the golden boy had a dream that he was out hunting and giving chase to a fine stag and when he awoke he said to his bride, 'I must go out and hunt.' She felt worried and begged him to stay at home saying, 'You may easily have some terrible accident.' But he replied, 'I must and will go.'

So off he went into the forest and before long a proud stag, just like the one he had seen in his dream, stopped in front of him. He aimed at it and was about to shoot when the stag sprang away. He chased after it over ditches and bushes without wearying the whole day. But

towards evening the stag disappeared before his very eyes and when the golden boy looked about him he found himself in front of a small house in which lived a witch.

He knocked at the door and a little woman came out and asked, 'What do you want so late at night in the middle of this great forest?'

He said, 'Haven't you seen a stag round about here?'

'Yes,' she replied, 'I know the stag well,' and just then a little dog which had come out of the house with her began to bark fiercely at the stranger.

'Shut up, you little wretch!' he cried, 'or I'll shoot you dead.'

'Are you intending to kill my dog!' cried the witch furiously and immediately cast a spell on him and turned him into stone so that he lay there motionless while his bride waited for him in vain and thought, Surely something evil has happened to him and that was what lay so heavily on my heart and made me so fearful.

At home, in the meantime, the other brother was standing near the golden lilies when suddenly one of them fell off. 'Good heavens!' he cried, 'some great disaster has befallen my brother. I must set out and maybe I can help him.' But his father said, 'Stay here, for if I should lose you too, what would become of me?' But the son replied, 'I must and I will go.'

So he mounted his golden steed and rode away till he came to the forest where his brother, now turned to stone, lay. The old witch came out of her house and called to him and would have cast her spell on him too but he kept his distance and called out, 'I will shoot you down now if you do not restore my brother to life.' Very unwillingly the witch stirred from the spot and touched the stone with her finger. Immediately it took on its human life and the two golden youths rejoiced at seeing one another again; they kissed and hugged each other and then together rode out of the forest, one to return to his bride, the other home to his father.

'I knew you had saved your brother,' said the father, 'for all of a sudden the golden lily raised its head again and burst into bloom.' And from then on they all lived happily till the end of their days.

The Golden-Fleeced Ram and
the Hundred Elephants

There was once a young man called Marko who was lucky enough to own a very handsome ram with a golden fleece. Now it so chanced that the king of the country passed through Marko's village, and he saw the golden-fleeced ram and set his heart on it. But instead of setting about matters in a straightforward way and asking Marko if he would sell him the ram, or let him have it as a gift – which Marko might well have done, for he was a good-natured young man – the king asked the advice of his prime minister Milosu, who was Marko's uncle.

Milosu had always disliked his nephew, and he thought this would be a first-class chance to get rid of him and take his farm.

'Set the young man some impossible task,' he said to the king. 'Then when he fails you can chop his head off and take the ram.'

The king listened to this bad advice.

He sent for Marko and told him, 'You must plant me a vineyard and bring me wine from it in seven days. Otherwise I shall have your head cut off.'

Poor Marko was very upset. He wandered out of the village and up the mountain, weeping and wondering what he could possible do. When he had gone some distance from the houses he met a mysterious little girl, who suddenly appeared from behind a rock, and said,

'Why are you weeping, my brother?'

'Oh, leave me alone!' he snapped. 'Go your way, in God's name. My trouble is nothing to do with you, and you certainly can't help me.'

'Maybe I can, just the same,' she said. 'There's no harm in telling me.' And she persisted until he said, 'Oh, very well,' and told her what was worrying him.

'Why, I think we can do something about that,' said the little girl. 'I don't think that is too much of a problem. Go back, have the vineyard marked out, and order it to be trenched in straight lines. Now take these twigs of basil, put them into a sack, and for seven nights you must sleep lying between the trenches of the vineyard, with your head pillowed on the sack.'

And the mysterious little girl picked a bunch of the sweet mountain basil, with its grey leaves like smoke, and gave it to Marko. As he could think of no better plan, he did what she told him. He ordered the land to be dug and trenched, he put the basil-sprigs in a sack, and for seven nights slept between the trenches.

On the first morning he found the vines ready planted; on the second morning the leaves had begun to sprout; on the third the vines had grown tall; on the fourth morning they were in flower; on the fifth morning small grapes had begun to form; on the sixth morning the grapes were large and green; on the seventh morning the grapes were ripe and ready for picking.

Since it was the golden-fleeced ram the king really wanted, he was not at all pleased when Marko came before him on the seventh day with a jug of sweet wine and a cluster of grapes in his handkerchief.

'Never mind,' said the wicked uncle Milosu. 'That plan didn't work, but now we'll find him something really impossible to do. Tell him to build a tower out of a hundred elephants' tusks.'

Marko heard this order with despair. 'Why,' he thought, 'in this country it is uncommon to see even one elephant; how can I ever expect to find a hundred?'

And he wandered out of the village and up the wild mountain, with tears running down his cheeks.

He had not gone very far when the mysterious little girl suddenly appeared again, from the dry gully of a mountain stream.

'Why are you weeping, my brother?'

'Oh, what use is it to tell you?' he said. 'This time it is quite impossible that you should be able to help me.'

'Oh well, you never know,' said she. 'In any case you might just as well relieve your mind by talking the matter over.'

So Marko told her that he had been ordered to build a tower out of elephants' tusks.

'Oh, I do not think that is an impossible task,' said the mysterious child. 'What you must do is this: go back to the king and ask for three hundred barrels of wine and three hundred barrels of brandy. Have men with oxen drag the barrels up the mountain to a lake with a narrow outlet. Pour all the wine and brandy into the lake, and make a dam so that it cannot escape. Then many elephants will come to drink from the lake, and they will become drunk and fall down. Have carpenters ready to cut off their tusks; then, at the spot where the tower is to be built, you must lie down and sleep for seven nights with your head pillowed on the sack of basil. On the seventh day the tower will be ready.'

This time Marko believed the mysterious child; he went to the king and asked for three hundred barrels of wine and three hundred barrels of brandy, and for oxen to drag them up the mountain and men to dam up the lake.

Sure enough, when they had dammed the lake and poured in all the wine and brandy from the barrels, hundreds of elephants came hasting through the mountains, having smelt the liquor from many miles away. They came down to the verge of the lake, and drank and drank.

The wine and brandy made them joyful and they began to dance, waving their long trunks and fanning each other with their great ears. They trumpeted gaily, and the ground shook, so that the people in the king's city trembled and thought the mountain must be falling down.

Marko watched the elephants dance and he thought to himself. Why should these happy creatures lose their tusks so that the king may have an ivory tower? What have they done to deserve such a fate?

And he pulled out the keystone of the dam. Down rushed all the wine and brandy, straight down the side of the mountain so that the king and his palace and his wicked minister Milosu were all swept

away. But the elephants went gaily dancing and trumpeting away over the mountains, through Romania and Georgia, through Turkey, Iran and Afghanistan, until they came to their native land. And Marko went with them, riding on the largest elephant.

As for the golden-fleeced ram, it escaped up the mountain, who knows where?

As for the mysterious little girl, she was never seen again.

Linda-Gold and the Old King

L ong, long ago there lived an old king who was rather eccentric. People said he was odd because he had had many sorrows, poor old king. His queen and children had died, and he himself said his heart had been torn apart. Who had done that and how it had happened, he never told; but it was someone with claws, he said, and since then he imagined that everyone had claws on his hands.

No one was allowed to come nearer than two arms' lengths to the king. His valets were not allowed to touch him, and his dining-room steward had to place his food at the very edge of the table. The king had not shaken anyone's hand for many, many years. If people were careless enough not to remember about the two arms' lengths, and came an inch closer, the king had them put in irons for a week to refresh their memory.

In all other ways, the old king was a good king. He governed his subjects well and justly. Everyone was devoted to him, and the only thing his people regretted was that he had not found a new queen, or appointed anyone, prince or princess, to inherit the realm. When they asked him about this, however, he always said, 'Show me someone who does not have claws, and I will let that person be my heir.'

But no one ever appeared who, in the king's mind, did not have claws. The claws might be under the fingernails, or curled in the palm, but they were always there, he believed.

Now one day it happened that the old king was walking alone in the forest. He grew tired and sat down to rest on the moss and listen to the birds singing in the trees. Suddenly a small girl rushed up the path, her hair streaming behind. And when the king looked up, he saw in the trees a shaggy grey beast with flashing eyes and a grinning red mouth. It was a wolf, who wanted the little girl for breakfast. The old king rose and drew his sword, and straight away the wolf turned in fear and ran back into the forest.

When the wolf had gone, the little girl began to weep and tremble. 'Now you must walk home with me, too,' she said, 'or else the wolf will chase me again.'

'Must I?' asked the king, who was not accustomed to taking orders.

'Yes. And my mother will give you a loaf of white bread for your trouble. My name is Linda-Gold, and my father is the miller on the other side of the forest.'

What she said was right, the king decided. He couldn't very well let her be killed by the wolf, and so he was obliged to accompany her.

'You go first,' he said 'I will follow behind you.'

But the little girl did not dare walk first. 'May I hold your hand?' she asked, and moved closer to him.

The king started, and looked closely at the little hand raised to his. 'No, I am sure you have claws, too, though you are so small,' he said.

Linda-Gold's eyes filled with tears, and she hid her hands behind her back. 'My father says that, when all I have done is forgotten to cut my nails.' She felt ashamed and looked at the ground. But then she asked if she might at least take hold of his mantle, and the king agreed to that. He simply could not make himself tell her to keep two arms' lengths away, for she was only a small child who would not understand.

So she skipped along beside him and told him of her cottage and all her toys. She had so many beautiful things she wanted to show him. There was a cow made of pine cones, with match sticks for legs; a boat made from an old wooden shoe, with burdock leaves for a sail; and then best of all was a doll her mother had sewn for her from an old brown apron and stuffed with yarn. It had a skirt made from the sleeve of a red sweater, and a blue ribbon at the neck, and her big brother had drawn a face on it with coal and put on a patch of leather for a nose.

[178]

It was odd, but the old king listened patiently to all her chattering, and smiled. He was sure the little hand had claws, yet he let it pull and jerk at his mantle as much as it wished. But when Linda-Gold and the king came to the highway, and the mill was not far away, the king said goodbye. Now Linda-Gold could go home by herself.

But Linda-Gold was disappointed. She did not want to say goodbye so soon. She clung to his arm and tugged it, and begged him. How could he *not* want white bread, which was so good? It couldn't be true that he did not want to look at her fine toys! She would let him play with her doll all the evening, if only he would come home with her. She would give him a present – the boat with the burdock-leaf sails – because he had saved her from the wolf.

When none of this helped, she at last asked the king where he lived.

'In the castle,' he said.

'And what is your name?'

'Old Man Greybeard.'

'Good. Then I will come to visit you, Old Man Greybeard.' And she took off her little blue checked scarf, and stood waving it as long as the king could see her – and he turned to look back quite often because he thought her the sweetest little girl he had met in a long time.

Even after he had returned to the castle, he still thought of Linda-Gold, wondering if she really would come to visit him. He was worried because she did not want to keep her little hands at a respectful distance, but he could not deny that he longed to see her.

The king was still thinking of Linda-Gold the next morning, and feeling sure that she would not dare venture out so far for fear of the wolf, when he heard a clear child's voice calling from the palace yard. He went to the balcony and saw Linda-Gold with a rag doll under her arm. She was arguing with the gatekeeper. She said she must speak to Old Man Greybeard about something very important.

But the gatekeeper just laughed at her and replied that no Old Man Greybeard lived there. Then Linda-Gold got angry. He mustn't say that, she insisted, for she herself knew very well Old Man Greybeard did live there. He had told her so himself.

Next she went up to a lady-in-waiting who had just come outside, and asked her advice. No, the lady-in-waiting had never heard of Old Man Greybeard, either, and she too laughed heartily.

But Linda-Gold did not give up. She asked the cook, she asked the steward of the household, and she asked all the courtiers, who had begun to gather in the courtyard to stare at her. She turned red in the face as they all laughed, and her lower lip began to tremble. Her eyes were full of tears, but she still maintained firmly in a clear voice, 'He must be here, because he told me so himself.'

The king called from his balcony, 'Yes, here I am, Linda-Gold.'

Linda-Gold looked up, gave a shout of joy, and jumped up and down in excitement. 'Do you see, do you see!' she called in triumph. 'I told you he was here.'

The courtiers could do nothing but stare in surprise. The king had to command twice that Linda-Gold be brought to him before anyone obeyed. Then it was no less a person than the royal court's Master of Ceremonies who led her to the king's chamber. When the door opened, Linda-Gold ran straight to the king and set her rag doll on his knee.

'I will give you this instead of the boat,' she said, 'because I thought that since you saved me from the wolf you should have the best thing of all.'

The rag doll was the ugliest, most clumsy little bundle imaginable, but the old king smiled as if he were quite delighted with it.

'Isn't she sweet?' asked Linda-Gold.

'Yes, very.'

'Kiss her, then.'

And so the king had to kiss the doll on its fearfully ugly mouth.

'Since you like her, you should thank me, don't you think?'

'Thank you,' said the king, nodding in a friendly way.

'That wasn't right,' said Linda-Gold.

'Not right? How should it be then?'

'When you say thank you, you must also pat my cheek,' said Linda-Gold.

And so the king had to pat her on the cheek; but it was a warm, soft little cheek, and not at all unpleasant to pat.

'And now –' said Linda-Gold.

'Is there something more?' asked the king.

'Yes, I would like to pat your cheek, too.'

Here the king hesitated. This was really too much for him.

'Because, you see,' Linda-Gold went on, 'I cut my fingernails,' and she held up both her small chubby hands for the king to see. He

had to look at them whether he liked it or not.

And truly, he could not see anything unusual on the pink finger-tips. The nails were cut as close as a pair of scissors could do it, and there wasn't the trace of a claw.

'You can't say I have claws now, Greybeard,' said Linda-Gold.

'No . . . hmm . . . well, pat me, then.'

Linda-Gold flew up on his lap and stroked the old sunken cheeks and kissed them, and soon a couple of tears came rolling down. It was so long since the old king had known love.

Now he took Linda-Gold in his arms and carried her to the balcony. 'Here you see the one you have always longed for,' he called to those in the courtyard.

A loud cry of joy broke out among them. 'Hurrah for our little princess. Hurrah! Hurrah!' they shouted.

Surprised and bewildered, Linda-Gold turned to the king and asked him what this meant.

'It means they like you because you have fine small hands which never scratch and have no claws,' he said. Then he kissed the two little hands so that everyone could see, and from below the people shouted again, 'Hurrah for our little princess!'

And that is how Linda-Gold became a princess and in the course of time inherited the realm of the old king.

Andvari's Gold and the Curse of the Ring

One day Odin, father of the ancient Norse Gods, came down to visit Midgard to see how men fared there. Disguised in his cloud-blue cloak with his broad-brimmed hat pulled down over his missing eye, Odin and his two companions, Honir his brother and the cunning Loki, wandered the earth through woods and paths and just as the sun was setting they reached the gurgling waters of a rushing river.

Now this particular spot was the favourite haunt of Otter, son of Reidmar, the ancient king of the dwarf-people whose great Hall stood nearby. As he lay on the river bank on the look-out for fish, Otter's own shape was changed into that of a true river otter and he began to feed on a silvery trout which he had deftly snapped up in his snout.

The mischievous Loki, ever the one to start trouble, picked up a stone from the bank of the river where the three gods were resting and, flinging it at the otter, killed it with one blow.

'Aha!' cried Loki triumphantly, 'an otter and a trout with a single stone.' And he displayed his double catch to his admiring companions. 'This will pay for our night's lodging – and look, there it is.' Ahead of them the gods could see a grand hall from the roof of which smoke curled up into the sky.

[183]

It was a truly wondrous mansion, wrought with great craft and skill, set in a veritable forest of pillars and adorned with golden hangings. In the centre of the hall sat Reidmar arrayed in garments of purple as though woven from the dark ocean itself. His piercing eyes were deep set in a face of grim coldness and a majestic beard almost covered his body.

He first welcomed the visitors and entertained them with strange music and feasting. Yet even as they made merry the wanderers felt they were caught in a trap. For Reidmar's welcoming smile soon changed to scorn when Loki showed him the catch he had made of an otter and trout with one single stone and which he offered to Reidmar as payment for their night's lodging.

Reidmar's grim features now assumed a fearsome expression. Summoning his sons, Fafnir and Regin, he bade them bind the three gods in chains. 'Behold,' he exclaimed, 'these evil men have slain your brother.'

'But where, pray, is this brother whom you claim we have slain?' they asked in wonder. 'We have seen no one and killed no one. Of what do you accuse us?'

Then Reidmar pointed to the dead otter in Loki's hands. '*He* was my son. Know that I am Reidmar, master of black magic. Like me, my sons can change their shape at will – and most of all my son Otter, who loved to fish for hours on end in the stream close to Andvari's Fall, would assume the otter's shape the better to trap the fish as they leapt into the waterfall. And now you have killed him and for this – the death of my son – you shall pay with your lives.'

'But why kill us,' protested Honir, 'when we can offer you wer-gild payment for a killing which occurred by accident? Our friend here threw a stone at what he thought to be a true otter of the river. Come, come, my Lord, let justice be done and name the wer-gild price for your son's regrettable death.'

Reidmar laughed mockingly, the glint of greed and vengeance in his eyes, 'Heed me,' he cried. 'You may go free from here only when you have given sufficient gold to fill Otter's skin and enough to cover it so that not one single hair on his body be visible. Let him who slew my son go gather it while you two remain here in chains as hostages. If he fails to return with the gold, then you, his companions, will die at sunset tomorrow.'

So Loki left. Now he had to summon all his wits to find the gold –

the ransom demanded by Reidmar. He knew that the richest store of the precious metal was hoarded by Andvari, the dwarf-king, who guarded it with his very life, behind that self-same waterfall where Loki had caught the otter, cause of all their present woes. As he drew near the rushing waters, which men called Andvari's Force, a glimmer of gold reflected in the roaring stream, coming from the cave behind, caught his eye.

But where was Andvari himself?

Loki knew well the magical powers of Andvari, who could change himself at will to any shape or form. Nor could Loki hope to catch him with his bare hands. But Loki was nothing daunted. Resourceful as ever, he procured from Ran, the sea-giantess, the net she used to ensnare shipwrecked mariners.

Once he had glimpsed Andvari in the moonlight, swimming around and looking for all the world like a pike, he bided his time till the darkened waters allowed him to cast his net unseen, and indeed it was not long before Andvari, the pike, was entangled in Loki's cunning snare enmeshed in its cords.

Andvari groaned but Loki held fast till the dwarf-king returned to his own shape; he glared balefully at his hunter.

'I know why you have come,' he said, 'but that gold belongs to me, gathered by the sweat of my own hands and never, never will I surrender one grain of it to you.'

But Loki still held him in a grip of iron and said in a voice full of menace, 'I am Loki, the master of guile, Loki, the greatest of all shape-changers. And I will turn myself into a ravening lion and tear you limb from limb, and when you are no more, I shall seize the gold for myself.' Then Andvari knew that he was beaten and, like a defeated animal, crept to his lair, fetched out all the gold, heaping pile upon pile before Loki's gloating gaze. There was such a superabundance of the gleaming metal as had never been witnessed by the eye of god or human.

Greedily sweeping it all up into his net, Loki was still quick enough to glimpse from the corner of his eye Andvari's hand about to retrieve a golden ring from the pile. It was indeed a jewel of the greatest rarity, cunningly wrought with intertwining venomous snakes.

'Stay!' shouted Loki, pouncing upon him, 'not one speck will you retain.'

Andvari let out a cry of agony, 'Let me keep just this one ring,' he begged, 'for with it I can create more gold.' Loki snarled back at him, 'Every scrap of this gold I *will* have, including that ring.'

'Then take the ring, confound you,' cried Andvari wailing with grief and frustration, *'and may its heavy curse accompany it, for it will bring nothing but disaster to all who wear it – until both ring and gold return to their home in these waters.'* And Andvari glowered fiercely at the master of guile and he seemed to grow huge and grim as though an immense anguish swelled within him. And he remembered the prophecy of the Norns who shape the fate of men and gods – the prophecy that declares that *to those wise beings who fashion the world, gold is the seed of further gold and unseen glory, but to wasteful men it is the seed of woe and grief to generations yet to come.*

'Heed me well,' he cried, 'for entangled in my gold are terrors untold. Kings will be slain and many a queen's heart will be broken. Two brothers and a father will be slain by my grief. This day will remain a day of great mourning to all.'

But Loki laughed silently for he knew that the curse would fall not upon himself but upon Reidmar. Then with all the swiftness of a god, he returned to Reidmar's Golden Hall. And when the vast hoard of gold was set down, it was as though the sun had left the heavens and made its home within its walls.

Now Odin had spotted the exquisite ring amidst the dazzle of the heaped treasure and slipped it on to his finger, thinking that Loki had brought more than enough gold to fill the otter's skin and cover every hair.

Reidmar and his two sons set about filling dead Otter's skin till it fairly bulged and could take no more. Then they greedily snatched up every scrap of the metal and covered his entire hairy hide until it sparkled and gleamed in the sunlight.

'Now, Reidmar, our debt is discharged and we can go free,' announced Odin.

'Not so fast,' said Reidmar, hoping to have both the gold and his captives' blood. But at that moment Reidmar's eye was caught as though by a blinding sunbeam from the other end of the hall. He had espied the ring on Odin's finger and with a look heavy with menace he cried, 'You will indeed die, for one hair of my dead Otter remains uncovered.'

Then Odin pulled the ring from his finger and covered the hair on the snout.

Regin loosened the shackles of the gods and they departed into the night. But as they left the hall, Loki shouted back: 'WITH THAT RING GOES ANDVARI'S CURSE WHICH WILL BRING SORROW AND MOURN- ING TO ALL WHO WEAR IT.'

Indeed the Ring began its deadly work immediately and evils followed swiftly one upon the other.

Reidmar remained transfixed where the gods had left him in the hall, still gazing in triumphant unbelief at the immense treasure of gold which was now his. Nor did he heed his two sons, Fafnir and Regin when they said, 'Father, let us now share out this booty. We too have been wronged. Otter was our brother and without our help you would not have won the gold.'

'Not one grain of this metal will you have,' said Reidmar, spreading himself all over the gleaming treasure, as if to protect it with his own body. Then Fafnir, in uncontrollable fury, picked up an axe and with one mighty blow cut off his father's head. And the gold was drenched with Reidmar's blood.

And as his brother Regin looked at him he saw him change visibly before his eyes. Fafnir's hands were gory with the blood of the father he had murdered, and in a voice which chilled Regin's heart with terror, he snarled, 'Yes, I have in truth slain my own father so that I alone may keep this gold. Nor will I give you one tiny piece. I shall dwell alone and brood over my gold.'

As he spoke his face grew more awful to look upon. After a while as Regin dared to lift his eyes, he met a sight too monstrous to describe. The hideous creature he now saw was carrying off all the treasure hoard of Andvari's gold to hide it in a cave remote from the reach of mortal men.

And this was the last time he saw his brother in human shape. For when he called out 'Fafnir' through the opening of the cave, an enormous dragon with bulging eyes rolling from side to side could be seen spreading its vast scaly body as a protective shield across the piles of gold. The stench of its foul breath permeated the air and Regin could scarcely breathe for terror. He fled in horror; fled from Fafnir the dragon; fled from the hoard of gold and fled from the glorious house which he himself had built with his own hands. He was now as poor as the day he was born and all that he had left was his heart which remembered all things and his skilled hands which were never still.

So Regin wandered the kingdoms of men brooding on revenge and vowing to himself that one day he would find the great hero who would slay the dragon for him. At last he came to the Kingdom of King Ilf, who, he had heard, was the friend of Sigmund the Volsung, the greatest of all warriors. And Regin became the King's smith. To Sigmund it was that the god Odin had given an enchanted sword.

Now who was this hero Sigmund and whence did he come?

The Volsungs

Long ago King Volsung sat on his throne in the Great Hall in the shade of the wondrous Branstock tree. A sumptuous banquet had been prepared to greet King Seggeir, the Goth King, who had come to claim as his bride King Volsung's daughter, the fair Signy.

As they feasted round the Branstock, suddenly a mighty man strode into Volsung's dwelling. His single eye shone out from under a broad-brimmed hat. His body was enveloped in a gleaming cloud-blue kirtle. In silence he walked up to the Branstock and drew from his kirtle a flashing sword which he drove deep into the tree. Then he spoke.

'Here in this Branstock lies a sword wrought of the finest steel. Let any man among you pluck it from the oak and it shall be his – a gift from me.' Then Odin departed.

All the guests sat silent for they knew that the sword would be the envy of all Midgard.

Then up spoke King Volsung, 'Arise, Earls of Goth and children of Volsung. Set your hands to the sword-hilt.'

King Seggeir was the first to approach the tree. Laying his hands on the hilt he pulled with all his strength. But in vain did he strive and pant, the sword remained embedded in the wood. His face purple with anger, he returned to his high seat. They have brought me here to mock me, he thought, but I will make them pay dear.

Then the Earls of the Goth folk and the Volsung men, every single one tried his hand, but for all their efforts Odin's gift remained fast in the oak. Last of all came Volsung's youngest son, Sigmund. With a seeming gentle tug he freed the blade from the enchanted tree and held the naked weapon high above his head before the unbelieving eyes of the onlookers. There was a shattering roar of acclamation as Sigmund stood briefly before them.

Then Seggeir's heart was choked with envy, but putting on a sickly smile he said, 'Sigmund, son of Volsung, happy am I for the glory you have gained. But there is something even more glorious to be won. If you deign to give me that sword so freely drawn, I can offer you untold gold from my storehouse, and silver and amber too.'

Sigmund replied, laughing in scorn, 'Not even twice that treasure will buy from me Odin's sword that not even the might of kings could wrest from the Branstock.'

Seggeir's face turned pale but feigning a smile he said, 'I respect your honour even as I respect my own.' But in his heart Seggeir swore vengeance for the great slight he had suffered.

When King Volsung and his sons and Earls came, at Seggeir's invitation to his kingdom, where Signy, Volsung's daughter was now Queen, Seggeir's vow was fulfilled. King Volsung was taken by surprise, and Seggeir's men, the Goth folk, emerged in great numbers – an army of bristling spears and fell upon the unsuspecting Volsungs, killing them all. King Volsung's sons, bound in chains, were thrown to the mercy of the wolves. Sigmund alone survived, though robbed of Odin's sword. He burst his chains asunder and gripping the wolf by the throat he slew his adversary with his bare hands. He knew then that all pity had died in his heart and henceforth he would live only to have revenge on the Goth King who had besmirched the name of the gods and honour of the Volsungs.

Signy, his sister, Queen to the wicked Seggeir, secretly smuggled the precious sword out to him. Sigmund fell upon the guards and slew them; then he hastily collected a pile of faggots and set fire to Seggeir's Hall. Sigmund cried out, 'Just punishment is meted out by the hand of Sigmund the Volsung.'

It was then that Signy appeared arrayed in her queenly robes. 'My kin have been avenged and Sigmund has brought glory to the great name of Volsung.' But this was the last time that Signy was seen by mortal men for she turned into the flames and vanished.

Sigmund returned to the great Hall of the Branstock where he sat enthroned among its boughs and there he reigned as the mightiest and most just King of all Midgard.

Sigmund Weds Hiordis

Far away from the Kingdom of Volsung lived King Elymi, whose beautiful daughter Hiordis was wooed by many suitors. Her father had promised that she should wed only the man of her own heart's choice and now the fair lady had to choose between King Sigmund, whose valour and goodness were universally known, and King Lyngi, a young and handsome neighbour, smooth-lipped but treacherous of heart.

Hiordis wasted little time in making up her mind. 'Pray tell King Sigmund', she said, 'that I deem it the highest honour to be his Queen.'

Now Sigmund was warned that King Lyngi was sure to challenge him in battle for he was smitten with jealousy that he had not been chosen by Hiordis. And so it was that not many months after the wedding of Sigmund and Hiordis, when the Volsung men were preparing to return to their kingdom with their new Queen, news came of mighty armies coming ashore along the coasts of King Elymi's realm. They were the dreaded soldiery of King Lyngi, vengeance-bound to slay his enemy. Sigmund and Elymi, followed by their armies, rode down to the sea strand and all too soon found themselves in combat with their foe.

Queen Hiordis, with one of her maidens, ascended a wooded slope to view the battle scenes. She saw King Sigmund in the forefront of his army – a majestic figure gleaming in the noonday sun and the whole earth seemed to tremble as the hosts of King Lyngi ran upon the Volsungs and the men of Elymi's islands as would wolves upon their prey.

But at the point of Sigmund's greatest glory, when his voice rang out with the ancient song of his kinsmen and he thought that ere long he would sit triumphant as King of Midgard, there appeared, unexpected, in front of the bristling enemy swords, a one-eyed man whose face shone like a flame from under his broad-brimmed hat. He was robed in a cloud-blue cloak and carried a mighty double-bladed sword which he raised in contest with Sigmund's sword of the Branstock – his own gift to the Volsung King. Then the blue-clad figure, which was Odin himself, vanished and the enemy weapons drove against Sigmund and drove him down and both his men and the army of King Elymi were vanquished.

As for Hiordis, when all the enemy had departed, she made her way with heavy heart towards the heaps of dead on the battle-field. She did not have to go far before she found her Lord dying among a pile of warriors he himself had slain. Hiordis tried to comfort him, saying, 'As long as you are still breathing the leeches can heal you.'

'No,' said Sigmund, 'I must obey the will of Odin. I have seen him today, though he said no word to me. But before I go to my last resting place, let me tell you of things yet to come which may be of some solace to you. Yonder, where I fought, lie the shards of my sword which Odin gave me. Go gather them, for today Odin has taken from me the gift he once gave. A *better than I* will arise to tell the tale and it is for him that these shards must be smithied; and he shall be my son to do what I have left undone. He shall be the noblest of all the heroes of Midgard.'

Sigmund spoke no more. All night he lay dying and not until the sun rose over the sea did he breathe his last.

Hiordis looked up and espied a ship of war heading swiftly for the shore. She sped away to the thicket where her maid awaited her. 'My Lord is dead,' she said, 'and here we are, two lonely women, and earls from overseas approaching. Let me don your blue gown and you will take my purple and gold and wear my crown on your head. You will say you are King Sigmund's Queen and I will say that I am your handmaid.' And there and then they exchanged their raiment.

The Lord of these incoming seamen was King Ilf and as he stood by the tiller in the cold light of dawn, he beheld the destruction left after the mighty battle. And to his amazement he saw one lone woman, a crown upon her head, running swiftly away. King Ilf gave the order to land and having waded through the confusion of slain warriors, he came upon the body of Sigmund.

'Look upon this,' said King Ilf, 'for here lies a mighty Lord. Would that I were of his kindred, for there is not his like left in Midgard, and Odin has claimed him this day for Valhalla. Now let us seek the woman who seemingly was fleeing to the woods. Maybe she will tell us the tale of this mighty battle.'

Soon they found not one but two women and spoke kindly to them. The gold-crowned 'handmaid' said, 'I am Queen Hiordis and King Sigmund lying there on the battlefield was my Lord.' King Ilf asked, 'Who then is this blue-eyed maiden, like a goddess in her loveliness?'

'This is my serving maid,' came the answer, 'and we are in dread of our lives.' King Ilf gazed hard at her but said no more. Then they all returned to the field of death and set to work to raise a mound for Sigmund. But in vain did they look for the scattered shards of Sigmund's sword. Then Hiordis herself, in the guise of her serving maid, spoke. 'King Sigmund bade that the shards of the sword given him by Odin be borne to our Lady Queen.'

Then King Ilf invited the two women to take refuge in his realm and on their arrival they were presented to the old Queen, mother of Ilf. She stared long at them and wondered why the less noble-looking was attired more richly than her mistress. She asked her son to speak to them and watch them unawares. One day he asked the gold-clad one how it was that she always seemed to awake with the dawn. She replied that ever in her youth she awoke at daybreak to milk the cows and drink the whey and since then, even in the pitch darkness of winter, her thirst awoke her. Strange it seemed to King Ilf that a princess had need to rise at dawn to milk the cows, so he turned to the handmaid for she appeared the more queenlike of the two and asked the same question. 'My father', she replied, 'gave me the gold ring which I still wear and it has the enchanted power of becoming ice-cold at first light.'

Then King Ilf was in no doubt that the two women had exchanged roles and that Hiordis was the real Queen, the wife of Sigmund. And it was plain to all that she was soon to bear a child. She told the King that Sigmund was the father of the expected child and that she had changed roles with her maid, lest the enemy, King Lyngi, should find her and force her to be his Queen.

Then Ilf declared his love to Hiordis and that very night she sat on the throne, the crown on her head, and dreamt of all that had been and of all that was to be.

Regin and the Birth of Sigurd

In the Hall of King Ilf lived Regin – that selfsame Regin, son of Reidmar and brother of Fafnir, that gold-besotted dragon who guarded his treasure on the Glittering Heath. Long, long ago, Regin had fled from his dragon brother in terror of his life and after years of wandering, nursing his grievances and brooding only on revenge, he had arrived at last at King Ilf's court where he became the King's master smith.

And now, there had come to this land the fair Hiordis whom Ilf had made his Queen. And it was here that her son was born.

The boy had eyes of such remarkable brightness that his mother spoke to him as though he understood her words, and she told him of his father, Sigmund the Volsung, of his woes and of his joys.

When the news of his birth was brought to King Ilf his joy knew no bounds. 'Oh, Sigmund!' he cried, 'my heart was stricken when I beheld you among the fallen warriors but now it is lifted by the birth of your son.'

And Ilf and Hiordis named the boy Sigurd. And his name was echoed through street and market and rang out over meadow and forest. And the hearts of everyone were stirred.

As the boy grew to be strong and wise so too grew the hopes in Regin's heart that here was the great hero who alone could be the dragon-slayer he had so long awaited, but he bided his time.

Regin addressed King Ilf: 'I fostered you in your youth, Your Majesty, and now the time has come when I must foster Sigurd, for my heart tells me that his future days will be blessed with great glory.'

To which King Ilf replied, 'I would welcome you to do that, for all the skills I know have been taught to me by you. But I implore you, Regin, to withhold that especial guile that is solely yours. This son of Sigmund is most dear to my heart.'

'Have no fear,' said Regin, 'your word is my command.'

So Sigurd went to live with Regin who taught him all things: the art of writing and the tongues of many men, to play the harp and to use his voice in song. Sigurd slew many a wood-wolf and mountain bull as he grew strong both in mind and body.

But the heart of Regin was tormented, for, tinged with the fondness he felt for the boy was the gnawing at his heart for revenge and for Fafnir's gold. He began to goad Sigurd and spur him on to action. He tried to make him discontented with his lot, persuading him that he lacked advancement. But Sigurd's heart and soul were loyal to his stepfather and he would have none of Regin's sinister suggestions. 'My father loves me as I love and honour him,' he said, 'and I have but to ask and he will grant me anything.'

'Then why', asked Regin, 'have you no horse you can call your own? Go ask your father for one of his horses, the best he has. That will be the true test of his love for you.'

Sigurd asked his father if he could choose a horse, an untamed colt that he could train as his own.

'Yes indeed, Sigurd,' replied the King. 'Take whichever horse you fancy, he shall be yours, with my blessing. May he be worthy of you.'

At dawn the following day Sigurd went down to the meadows where the horses grazed. As he made his way a man of ancient bearing, with a broad-brimmed hat pulled over his unseeing eye and clad in a cloud-blue cloak, stepped out in front of him. 'What brings you here, young sir?' he asked of Sigurd. To which Sigurd replied, 'Your face, good sir, shines like those battle-eager warriors of whom my master Regin has spoken. Your bearing fills me with awe. Pray tell me how I should choose the noblest steed in the meadows.' 'First,' replied the old man, 'we must drive the horses to the water's edge and we shall see what happens then.'

Then they both drove the horses till they came to a rushing river. The whole herd of horses ran into the river but the flood was too strong for them. Some were swept downward, some were caught in the eddies and sank in the swirling hubbub. But one, only one, a great grey stallion, swam across. They saw him toss his mane as he reached the flowery meadow.

Then the ancient one spoke again. 'I once gave to your father a rare gift, which you may yet consider precious, and this horse, which has outstripped the rest, is my gift to you. Ride him well for he is of the blood of Sleipnir. Greyfell is his name and there is no horse like him anywhere on earth.' With these words the stranger vanished.

And Sigurd knew that he had that day seen and spoken to Odin, father of the gods, who rides across the skies on Sleipnir, the eight-legged horse that Loki had given him.

The grey horse swam to the shore and leapt lightly on to the dry land. He seemed to sense that Sigurd was his master, so glad was he to be mounted by him. And Sigurd burst into joyous song as he rode along on his back.

Regin Tells the Story of Fafnir the Dragon

Regin knew now that the moment had come. Sigurd was full grown, a strong and handsome man, much loved by the people. It was then that Regin told him the tale that had never been told before: how the gods came down to earth and how Loki had slain his brother, Otter. Then Sigurd heard from Regin the terrible story of the hoard of gold now guarded by the fearsome dragon, Fafnir, who lay spread out over it in the cave on the Glittering Heath, protecting it with his monstrous body. Regin's story continued: 'So deadly is its venom that no hero has dared venture against it.'

'I will dare,' cried Sigurd. 'I will slay Fafnir the dragon. Sigurd the Volsung will be Fafnir's bane. But first I must have a sword fit for the mighty deed. Master Smith, pray fashion me a sword the like of which has never been and never will be.'

Then Regin bent over his work-bench and wrought his magic skills to fashion a shining sword, but when Sigurd swung it over his head and brought it down with all his might on the anvil, it shattered to a thousand pieces.

'Ah Regin,' exclaimed Sigurd, 'are you mocking me? Do you intend that I should go like a lamb to the slaughter with so weak a sword?'

Then Regin worked the whole night and forged a second sword which Sigurd gazed at with admiration but when he tested it the sparks and fragments scattered all over the forge; in Sigurd's hand only the hilt remained intact.

The Forging of the Sword of Wrath

The next morning Sigurd went to his mother and told her that Regin had twice attempted to fashion him a sword and twice had failed. 'Such swords are not for me, the son of Sigmund,' he cried. 'Pray, mother give me the shards of Sigmund's sword, gathered that night when he was slain in battle, for I long to do those deeds for which the sword is destined.' Then Hiordis knew that the time had come for Sigurd to prove himself.

Hand in hand they went to the Queen's treasure-house, where still gleaming brilliantly were the broken fragments of the hero King's sword with its gem-studded hilt. 'These', said Hiordis, 'are the shards I myself gathered at Sigmund's command, to hide them against the day when the man who was not yet born was ready. And now you stand before me, my own son, Sigurd the Volsung. Regin will re-fashion these shards and *you* will wield the sword, the gift of Odin, which your father alone was able to withdraw from the Branstock tree in the Great Hall of his father, King Volsung, many years since.'

Sigurd smiled with joy. 'Well have you guarded these shards,' he cried, 'and you do well to give them to me to fulfil the hopes laid upon them.' He kissed his mother and left.

Sigurd presented the shards to Regin. 'These are the remains of that glorious weapon my father wielded in his final battle. And these, re-fashioned, will be my sword. I implore you, master, to bring your unequalled skill to bear to this great task.'

Without delay Regin set to work to weld together the shards of Sigmund's sword and when it was done it had a mightier hilt than before and a living flame curled round the edge of the blade, making it seem like some enchanted mingling of sun and lightning. Then Sigurd girded the sword and exclaimed, 'I am armed with the Sword of Wrath and I am ready to ride to the Glittering Heath to rid the earth of the monstrous dragon!'

'But first I must leave you, Regin,' he continued, 'to carry out the deed which falls upon me alone. I can seek no glory till I have avenged my father's death. And when 'tis done as done it will be, then we two will start on our perilous journey – to seek out Fafnir the dragon in his foul lair.'

Then Sigurd, with a band of faithful followers, sailed across the seas to seek out his enemy, the cruel King Lyngi, who had slain his father in battle and when he met his hated foe he slew him with one single blow from his newly wrought sword.

Then Sigurd returned to his home where his people welcomed him as a great hero. His mother wept as she greeted him, saying, 'You, Sigurd my son, have restored honour to the name of Volsung.'

But he did not tarry long in his own land. The Norns (the Fates) had ordained that Sigurd and Regin be drawn to Fafnir's hoard of gold and the curse of Andvari's ring lay in wait to wreak further havoc. Side by side they rode out into the wilderness. Higher and higher rose the slope of the land but Regin threaded pathways through seeming impenetrable barriers. The darkness grew more intense. The moon had long since died and the stars were pale lightless dots. Would they ever see the light of day again? thought Sigurd. But there, at last, from the west, came the faintest glimmer of light, and then another and another, like tiny flashes of some distant fire. As they rode on, the light increased. Sigurd, straining his eyes, saw all around a land utterly bare and void. Then his heart lightened for he knew his journey had come to an end.

Sigurd Slays the Dragon

Sigurd leapt down from his horse and made his way through the dim light, prepared for the crucial encounter with his formidable foe. Regin kept well away on the pretext of protecting the horses from the dragon-beast, whose fiery breath would send them bolting away in terror.

As Sigurd advanced a cloud-blue shape emerged from the darkness, becoming larger and more solid as it approached, until it became the figure of a mighty man wearing a broad-brimmed hat down over his missing eye and smiling a friendly smile. 'Hail, Sigurd,' he began, 'I see you girt with the ancient sword and accompanied by your splendid steed. What is your destination?'

'The road I follow leads to the cave of Fafnir the dragon-king of the Hoard of Gold and I intend to deal him a deathly blow with my sword.'

'But first some words of advice,' said the stranger. 'As you reach your goal you will come to the track that leads to the rushing river where Fafnir comes down to slake his thirst. This is his track. You must dig yourself a tunnel pathway under this and lie in it as though dead, for this pit is destined to be Fafnir's grave.'

'I shall follow your counsel,' said Sigurd, but as he spoke he seemed to be talking to the air for the cloud-blue figure had vanished.

Then Sigurd knew that he had spoken to Odin, the god of gods.

He walked but a short distance when he came upon the dragon's track, gleaming like a silver ribbon in the moonlight. Sigurd shuddered, for the track marks left him in no doubt that he was about to face the most fearsome beast in all Midgard. But his horror soon gave way to triumphant joy, for had he not made this long trek to seek out the monster whose tracks he had now traced and had not great Odin told him that this was the very place where Fafnir's grave was to be dug? So Fafnir was the enemy of the gods and he, Sigurd, was their champion.

Then he began to dig the ground with great vigour, making a pit deep enough for him to strike upwards with his sword as he lay on his back. He slithered down into the tunnel and covered the top of the pit hole with loose branches which he had gathered beforehand. Then he lay like one dead, though fully alert, to wait till morning.

Dawn broke with Sigurd sensing the beast's approach. The earth around him trembled as the dragon's massive frame snaked its way down the track towards the river. Sigurd could hear his snorting breath and feel the steaming stench of his venom. But he could not see him for all was still dark around save the red tints in the sky peeping through the loose branches above him. The stench assailing Sigurd's nostrils was now so overwhelming that he thought he would faint, but his faithful sword remained steadily poised upward until scale after scale went clinking against the pointed blade. Sigurd's heart all but stopped as the deadly sword tip pierced the monster's soft underbelly, whereupon Sigurd instinctively thrust the weapon further upward with one superhuman effort; it sank into Fafnir's very heart leaving only the hilt exposed.

As the beast's red-hot blood gushed over Sigurd's head, a curse issued from the dying dragon's maw.

'May everlasting pestilence plague you, Sigurd the Volsung. For who but the son of Sigmund with his mighty Sword of Wrath could have dared to bring about my death? The name of Sigurd will henceforth be known as Fafnir's Bane. *And the curse of Andvari will be upon you.*'

Thus ended the most infamous life of that most foul and venomous monster. All was silent and the son of Sigmund stood still by the pool of Fafnir's blood. And the sun shone once again over the Glittering Heath; a light wind blew up and once more the air was fresh over the dread vastness. Sigurd cleansed himself of the monster's stinking gore and he stood there, proud in his armour of gold, his hair shining in the sun, his horse Greyfell now by his side.

Sigurd Slays Regin on the Glittering Heath

Regin now came to him, his eyes white with anger. He turned to the dead dragon, bent down and drank from the pool of blood, lapping it up like a dog. Wiping the blood from his lips he scowled at Sigurd and said, 'You have slain my brother.'

'True,' replied Sigurd, 'My deed and yours is now done. But henceforth our paths will diverge.'

Regin's brow darkened and his expression grew grimmer. He repeated, 'You have slain my brother, Sigurd. How will you atone for that?'

'Come now, master Regin,' retorted Sigurd, 'take all the gold which I have won for you and let us go our different ways.'

Regin repeated yet again, 'You have slain my brother. Today you become my slave to do whatever I command.'

Then with his bare hands Regin tore out the heart from Fafnir's breast as the eagles flew overhead with their shrill cries, watching the dead beast's entrails.

'Take this heart,' he said to Sigurd, 'and roast it for me that I may eat it and once more be your master. For in that heart lies the might and wisdom of all time.'

Then Sigurd took the heart and kindled a fire and sang as he roasted Fafnir's heart. The roasting seemed to take an exceedingly long time, while Sigurd, stretching out his hand, kept testing it to see if it was done. But the blood and fat seeped seething from the heart, scalding Sigurd's fingers, so that he put them in his mouth to still the pain. In doing so he tasted the flesh of the dragon and the blood of its heart. And then a great change came over him and, suddenly, he appeared to understand what the birds flying overhead were saying; and all the wisdom of the dwarf-folk flowed into his head. His eyes flashed as he listened to the voices of the eagles, understanding their speech. There were seven eagles in all and six of them cried out, telling him not to delay but to kill Regin, for he it was who had, with subtle cunning, planned Fafnir's death so that he, Regin, might fashion the world according to his own evil destiny. And the seventh eagle cried even louder that the rest. 'Arise, Sigurd,' it exclaimed, 'lest you be too late! Regin intends to murder Sigurd, so that he alone might be the possessor of Andvari's gold.'

Sigurd sprang to his feet and there before his astonished eyes stood Regin, knife in hand, poised to kill. Sigurd tried to stay Regin's hand. 'What is amiss, my friend?' he cried. 'I have roasted Fafnir's heart as you asked.' But Regin, in his madness, lunged forward to stab, and in the struggle to wrest the knife from him, Sigurd thrust him backward. Regin slipped, and the knife went instead into Regin. As his life ebbed away he cried out, 'the gold, the gold, THE CURSED GOLD HAS BEEN THE DEATH OF ME!'

Then Sigurd wept, for Regin, once his friend, was dead, hoist by his own petard; the pull of the gold and the desire for revenge had been tearing away at the heart of the smith all these years, and now it had come to this.

Sigurd ate the heart of Fafnir and, as he ate, the urge to achieve mighty deeds grew strong within him. He leapt on Greyfell and rode to the end of the heath to Fafnir's cave. He strode through the opening and saw before him golden armour, golden rings and even grains of golden sand. But amid all the treasure, Sigurd was struck most of all by the ring of the dwarf Andvari, resting like some bright star on the midmost heap. Sigurd slipped the ring – ignorant of its *curse* – on to his finger. The eagles flying overhead now urged him on to new adventures.